Two Against the Tide

Two Against the Tide

///

❧❧❧ BRUCE CLEMENTS

A Sunburst Book
Farrar, Straus and Giroux

Copyright © 1967 by Bruce Clements
All rights reserved
Library of Congress catalog card number: 67-19883
Published in Canada by Collins Publishers, Toronto
Printed in the United States of America
First edition, 1967
Sunburst edition, 1987

This book is for
Mark, and Ruth, and Martha, and Rachel,
with whom it is a privilege to live,
and for Hanna

❦❦❦❦ contents

Two Against the Tide

A Kidnapping?

"Never get into a car with a stranger." That was a fixed rule, never to be broken, and it kept going around in Tom's head as he stood next to the phone, worrying.

He had just come home from school a few minutes before. The first hour of his summer vacation wasn't over yet. Ahead of him stretched more than two whole months of freedom. He picked up the phone and started to dial his father's office number, but he stopped halfway through, put the phone down, and tried to remember exactly what Aunt Eve had said to him when she called.

"Hello, Tom. This is Aunt Eve."

Perfectly natural, ordinary, friendly words spoken by a familiar voice.

"Mom isn't here right now, Aunt Eve. She's out shopping all afternoon."

"Yes, I know, Tom. It's you I want to speak with. You know that your mother and father are planning to drive you and Sharon up to visit me next week. Well, there's been a change in plans. You're going to start your visit today instead of this Sunday. Sharon home yet?"

"Sharon? No, she isn't, but she'll be here in a little while."

"When she comes home, bring her downstairs with you and start walking toward Central Park. I'll come by in my car—it's a dark blue Chevrolet—and pick you up."

"Do Mom and Dad know?"

He had felt silly asking that question. Aunt Eve certainly wouldn't be calling him if she hadn't talked to his parents first.

"Everything's taken care of," she had answered right away. "And don't worry about packing. That's all been taken care of, too. All right?"

"I shouldn't bring anything at all?"

"Just yourself and Sharon."

"Well, I guess I'll see you in a little while, then."

"Good. I look forward to it, Tom. Goodbye."

"Goodbye, Aunt Eve."

That was the whole conversation. He remembered it perfectly. And he remembered the rule, too: Never get into a car with a stranger. But was Aunt Eve a stranger? He knew where she lived: Box 27, Northfield, Vermont. He had sent thank-you notes to her at that address five or six times a year for as long as he could remember. And every time she came to New York, which was once or twice a year, she always called to say hello. It was true he had never actually seen her, but that was because she was always too busy to come by.

He got up and went over to the piano. There, behind some other pictures, was a picture of Aunt Eve. He picked it up and looked at it closely for the first time in his life, hoping it would tell him something, but it didn't. It was just a glossy photograph of an old lady with a smile on her face.

It reminded him of another picture he knew, but he couldn't remember what the other picture was, or where he'd seen it. Written on the bottom in a fancy hand was: "To Barbara and Fenton. May you live happily ever after. Love, Aunt Eve." With the picture, which had arrived on his parents' wedding day, had come an envelope with ten fresh $100 bills in it. Ever since that day, Tom's mother and father had shared a special feeling for her.

The gift was especially surprising because Tom's mother hadn't seen Aunt Eve since, as a child, she

had spent her summer vacations on her grandmother's farm in Vermont. Eve Standish had been
one of her grandmother's friends, but younger and
livelier than her grandmother, and she knew how to
do all kinds of things. It was Eve Standish who had
taught Tom's mother how to knit, how to crochet,
how to make prints with linoleum blocks, and even
how to fish.

Then her grandmother had died. Shortly after the
funeral, Aunt Eve had bought the old farm for a
good price. No one had visited there since, partly
because there were too many other things to do,
partly because Aunt Eve seemed to be away a lot,
and mostly because she had never invited anyone,
until now.

Still, you couldn't say she was a stranger. She was
one of those eternal distant aunts, who aren't really
aunts at all, that almost everyone seems to pick up
on the way through life. The chief difference was
that Aunt Eve was a lot richer, and a lot more gener-
out, than most.

She never forgot birthdays, she never forgot Christmas, and she never forgot a wedding anniversary.
And the present she seemed to enjoy giving the most
was money, in large amounts: $15 or $20 for a birthday, a few hundred dollars for a wedding anniversary, $50 or $100 for Christmas, and odd amounts on
such days as Valentine's Day, and Mother's Day, and
Lincoln's Birthday. A person could depend on her.
No wonder, then, that Tom's mother and father called

her "Good old Aunt Eve," and "Sweet old Aunt Eve," and, occasionally, "Wonderful old Aunt Eve."

Tom studied wonderful old Aunt Eve's photograph and waited for Sharon to come home. He went into the kitchen, with the photograph in his hand, and looked at the clock over the stove. It was 3:47, a little past the time for Sharon to be home. He went back into the living room and put the picture down on the piano. He stood thinking.

"Maybe," he thought to himself, "I should bring just one or two little things with me." Aunt Eve lived on a farm. Should he bring a bat and ball, which might get lost in the tall pasture grass? Should he bring a flashlight? He didn't have a flashlight. Matches? No. How about his swimming suit? That was a good idea, but he didn't know where it was, and he wasn't a good swimmer, and he didn't want to hunt for it, and it might be too small for him since last year anyway. He looked back at Aunt Eve's picture. She looked very generous. He knew she'd buy him whatever he needed.

He heard a key in the door and heard the door open and turned to see Sharon come in. She was home. Good. He watched her as she walked over to the couch.

"Don't sit down, because we have to leave." Tom gave this order in what he felt was a very firm but at the same time very kind tone of voice. She sat down anyway.

"What do you mean?" she said.

"I mean we have to leave," Tom said, as if he had explained everything.

"Why?" Sharon asked, leaning back.

"There isn't time to explain it to you right now," he said. "We just have to go, that's all." As he said this, he walked toward the door, and when he got there Sharon was right behind him with a puzzled, unhappy expression on her face. Still, she was ready to follow him. That was exactly what he wanted from her once in a while, blind obedience, so while they stood waiting for the elevator in the hall outside their apartment, he began to tell her about Aunt Eve's phone call. By the time he was through, they were in the elevator on their way down.

"Oh," she said, "then it's all right." Tom didn't know whether this was a statement or a question, whether she was *telling* him it was all right or *asking* him if it was all right. The elevator stopped, and Tom got out, but Sharon didn't. Instead, she pushed the number 5 button to go back up again. He had already started across the lobby when the elevator door began to close behind him and he realized that Sharon was still inside. He turned around and ran back and jumped in just as the door slammed.

"Why'd you do that?" he asked.

"I can't meet Aunt Eve in my school dress. Really, Tom, I can't." She was quiet a moment, and then she said, almost to herself, "Besides, I don't like it."

"What do you mean, you don't like it?" Tom asked, but she didn't answer. She just took out her door key, which she wore on a long green ribbon around her neck, and stood waiting for the elevator to stop. It stopped, the door slid open, she stepped out, went down the hall, and unlocked the apartment door. Tom followed her in and sat down on the living-room couch while she went into her bedroom to change.

"You look fine," he called out to her. "Really. You look perfectly all right the way you are." She wasn't in the room, but he could see her anyway. A fine-looking girl, with the body of a country walker— lean and straight and graceful. Her eyes were clear, deep brown, like old amber, and they looked at things with interest and caution. She didn't just look *at* things, or people, she looked *into* them. She was the kind of girl it's hard to tell a lie to, partly because you wouldn't want to deceive her, and partly because those amber eyes would know right away that you were lying.

The face around her eyes was quite ordinary. Her ears looked like anyone else's ears, and didn't stick out too far, though they did stick out a little. Her lips were neither too thick nor too thin, her nose was bony but not too big, and her chin was a perfectly common ordinary human chin. She had almost black hair, which fell without a wave nearly to her waist. Sometimes she wore it loose, brushed back and held by a ribbon, and sometimes she braided it.

Always, however, when you looked at her face, you ended up looking at those wonderful eyes, which made her common and healthy face seem at the same time beautiful and fragile.

"Are you almost done?" Tom called, loudly.

She immediately came back into the living room, still wearing her school dress. "I've looked everywhere for my green dress and I can't find it."

"What are you worrying about, anyway? You afraid of being kidnapped or something?"

"No . . ." She went to the window and looked down toward the street below. "Let's call Dad," she said, still looking out.

Tom hated to see Sharon unhappy or uncertain, so he went over to her and made a suggestion that sounded good. "I'll tell you what. I'll call Dad and ask him, and if he says all right, we'll go. If he isn't in, we'll go and just look for Aunt Eve's car. If we see it, and Aunt Eve's in it, O.K. If it isn't her, we'll know because we've got her picture. All right?"

"All right," Sharon answered, reluctantly.

Tom went to the phone and dialed his father's number. A secretary answered and told him that his father had been called out of the office for the whole afternoon, which was somehow what Tom had expected to hear. Sharon was already halfway to the door before he had hung up the phone. That's the way she was. When she had agreed to do something that she didn't want to do, she always tried to get it over with in a hurry. Going to the dentist with her was like being in a race.

"How long do you think we'll be there?" she asked Tom in the elevator on the way down.

"Two weeks, I guess."

The elevator stopped, the door opened, and they walked across the empty lobby and out onto West Seventy-sixth Street. They turned left and started walking quickly toward the park, looking for a dark blue Chevrolet.

"Wouldn't it be funny if good old Aunt Eve came along and turned out to be a kidnapper?" Tom asked, trying to make a joke.

The idea was so ridiculous Sharon almost laughed.

Aunt Eve

A woman's voice called out to them from a dark blue, fairly new Chevrolet double parked four or five cars down from Central Park West.

"Sharon? Tom?"

Behind the wheel, smiling, sat Aunt Eve. It looked like Aunt Eve, anyway.

"Who else could it be if it isn't Aunt Eve?" Sharon asked herself as she looked, with doubt in her eyes, toward the woman in the car, trying to match her face with the photograph.

"I've been waiting for you."

She had a lovely voice, as smooth and comfortable as red velvet, the kind of voice that makes whatever it says sound true. She leaned over, still holding the steering wheel with her left hand, and opened the car door.

"Come in."

They got in, Sharon first because Tom was holding the door open for her. He slid in and pulled the door shut.

"Better lock it, Tom."

As he reached for the button to lock the door, Aunt Eve started down Seventy-sixth Street. She drove past the entrance to their apartment building and turned right at the corner, where Tom saw a boy he knew standing in front of the drugstore. The boy didn't see him.

"Did you leave a note for your parents?" Aunt Eve asked.

Panic suddenly hit him. He hadn't left a note. Aunt Eve had told him everything was "arranged," so he hadn't even thought of it. Sharon felt panic, too, but it was mixed with anger. She looked at Tom.

"Didn't you write a note?"

"No, I didn't think I had to."

"You were right, Tom," Aunt Eve said. "I just wondered if you had, that's all."

"Well, no. We could maybe call on the phone

later, after Mom gets home from shopping. . . . Maybe we ought to do that."

"No, that won't be necessary," Aunt Eve said. "I'll be talking to her soon enough myself." From the way she said it, it was clear that the subject of phoning home was closed, not to be opened again.

They drove on uptown in silence and heavy traffic. After a while, when they were on the highway going north through Westchester, she pulled off the road, turned off the motor, and looked at them both. "I'm glad to see you."

"We're glad to see you, too, Aunt Eve," Sharon said. She hadn't planned to say it. It just came out.

They could both see that she wanted to kiss them, but she didn't seem to be the kind of woman who would just start kissing somebody without asking permission first. Tom would gladly have let her, and gladly kissed her back, too—after all, a kiss doesn't cost anything, and it is friendly—but Sharon was sitting between them, so he didn't move. Sharon, too, was willing to be kissed, but she was in no hurry for it. Sitting still in a silent car and being looked at by a stranger made her feel uncomfortable. She stared straight ahead and tried to smile to show that she wasn't being unfriendly.

"Hungry?" Aunt Eve asked, picking up a picnic basket from the back seat and putting it on Tom's lap. "You can share this. I'm almost sure it will be enough, but if you're still hungry when it's gone, we'll stop and get some more." She started the motor again and drove on, going north steadily but without hurry. The traffic wasn't heavy any more, and the newly green trees on either side of the road, and the newly sprung grass, looked beautiful in the late afternoon sun. Aunt Eve began to hum a song, but stopped right away.

"We have a long ride ahead of us, children. We're going to an island and it will be sunrise when we arrive."

Sharon's heart stopped for a moment. An island? Did her parents know this woman was taking them to an island?

"I thought you had a farm," Tom said with just a trace of worry in his voice.

"I do have a farm, Tom. As a matter of fact, I have two, one in Vermont and one on the coast of Maine."

They waited for her to say some more, but she didn't, so they tried to eat. Once they got started, it wasn't hard at all. There was cold chicken, bread and butter, cookies, two containers of orange juice with straws, five or six apples, some green grapes, and a wad of paper napkins. They were both hungrier than they had thought, and when they were through, all they had left were three apples, a wad of paper napkins, and a lot of bones and stems and cores and crumbs. Aunt Eve stopped the car, gathered all the garbage up in a paper bag, got out, and threw the bag in a can by the side of the road.

"Do you mind trading places with me?" Sharon

asked Tom while Aunt Eve was still over at the
garbage can. "I feel squeezed sitting here in the
middle." Tom liked riding next to the window, but
he said "sure" anyway, opened the door on his side,
got out, closed it again, and walked around the front
of the car. Aunt Eve called to him as he was getting
back in from the driver's side, "Do you want to stop
here awhile and stretch your legs?"

"No, we're just changing places," he said as he
slid in under the steering wheel. So Aunt Eve came
back to the car, got in, and they drove on.

Staring at her out of the corner of his eye, and
hoping she wouldn't notice, Tom suddenly realized
who the photograph on the piano at home reminded
him of. It reminded him of the face of Grandma
Smith on the label of every can of Grandma Smith's
Old Style Creamed Corn—a face forever fixed in an
expression of blank sweetness by years of smiling at
everything and thinking about nothing.

And yet this woman didn't look at all like that
label, or like the picture on the piano at home. She
didn't look like Grandma Smith, or like Grandma
Anybody. Her face was, above all, the face of ex-
perience. There was no sweet, simple-minded gen-
erosity in it. Here was a woman who would not
smile at everything, who would not easily allow herself to be fooled, who knew what she was doing, and
why. She looked, he thought, like Sharon might look
after sixty or more years of a not entirely happy life.

Clearly, however, this *was* the same person whose

photograph was on the piano. The nose, the chin, the rather broad and high forehead, the sharp-cornered eyebrows, were all there. But the whole face, in life, was absolutely different. It was as if Aunt Eve and her photographer had purposely tried to produce a picture of her which would look as unlike her as possible. This woman was certainly the real Aunt Eve, he decided, but she was not the sweet old lady he had expected.

On the Barge

As they rode north through the night, Sharon began listing to herself all the reasons for not worrying about what was happening to her. First, she told herself that she shouldn't worry because Aunt Eve had treated them kindly. She hadn't forced them to do anything they didn't want to do. Second, she told herself that she shouldn't worry because Aunt Eve was an old friend of the family's, liked by her parents. Third, she told herself that she shouldn't worry because their visit with Aunt Eve had been planned for a long time. And fourth, she told herself that she shouldn't worry because Aunt Eve was acting in a normal and friendly way.

So, she had four very good reasons for not worrying.

But there were three things that didn't seem completely right. First, she wasn't going where she had expected to go. Second, she wasn't going when she had expected to go. And third, she was going without talking to her mother and father.

Conclusion? Everything was all right, but everything was also not all right. There was a great deal to be said for feeling good, but at the same time there was a great deal to be said for being scared.

What should they do? Jump out of the car and shout that they were being kidnapped the next time they stopped for gas? No, they couldn't do that. People did that sort of thing in the movies, not in real life. So, what should they do? Or should they do anything at all?

These questions kept going around and around in her mind until she got dizzy and stopped thinking altogether.

By now the sun had almost finished setting. One bright star was shining above the orange horizon. Sharon leaned her head against the window and watched the fields and farmhouses go by. Then, after a while, she fell asleep. When Aunt Eve noticed it, she stopped the car, got out, and woke Sharon up just enough to get her out of the front seat and onto the back seat, putting a small pillow under her head. She spread a blanket over her legs and pulled it up to her shoulders. Already Sharon was asleep again. Aunt Eve bent down and kissed her lightly on the forehead. She gave the kiss almost as if it were an apology. Then she got back in the car and started it moving again.

"How much longer will it be, Aunt Eve?" Tom spoke quietly.

"Quite a while. We're hardly past Boston. Are you sleepy?"

"No. What's it like on your island?"

"It's very peaceful, and I think it's very beautiful, but it's not my island. Forty-seven other people live there too."

"Have you lived there for a long time?"

"Yes."

"What's there?"

"Well, first of all there are people, then there are fields, and there are trees, a few farms, a tall hill to look out from, pretty houses, beaches, lots of grass, some woods."

"Is there a town or something?" he asked.

"Yes," she said, "a small village, with a general store and a drugstore and a newspaper office and a movie house."

They went on talking quietly as the orange left the sky and the pale moon made the clouds white again.

They began talking about New York, and Aunt Eve told him how it had looked thirty years ago. They talked about cars—she knew a lot more than Tom did about motors, and he thought that he knew quite a bit—and they talked about farming, and about Mark Twain, and about a lot of other things. Tom got that happy feeling that sometimes comes to people when they're talking quietly in an automobile late at night, a feeling of safety and closeness. After a long while their conversation stopped. Tom leaned back in his seat and fell asleep.

He woke up the moment Aunt Eve touched his shoulder. It seemed to him that he'd been asleep for less than a minute. The first thing he saw was the dashboard lights of the car. He had to squint and turn his head away, they seemed so bright. Then he smelled, and then he heard, the sea.

"I have to drive the car onto the ferry, Tom, and I'll feel better doing it if you two aren't in it." It was Aunt Eve's velvet voice, very near his ear. "You and Sharon will have to wait at this end of the dock."

He looked through the open door of the car and saw Sharon standing next to it in a long yellow raincoat and yellow rain hat. He quickly swung his legs, which were a little stiff, out of the car, and stood up on the dock. The water beside the dock was very black, the sky overhead clear and full of stars. The moon was down. It was chilly, almost cold, and a gusty wind was blowing off the sea.

"Put this on, Tom. Without it, you'll get soaked with spray once we start, and it will help keep you warm now."

Aunt Eve handed him a raincoat, got back into the car, and started the motor again. She drove slowly out to the end of the dock and disappeared down a steep ramp. The ramp clattered and groaned, and then there were some more sounds, like chains being pulled across a table and dropped onto the floor. A car door opened and closed, and then it was quiet.

"There must be some kind of boat waiting," Tom said.

"Are you going to get on it?" Sharon asked, whispering.

"Sure. Why not?"

Sharon didn't answer. "What did you talk about while I was asleep?"

"All kinds of things," Tom said. "If you'd been listening, you wouldn't worry so much. She's real nice."

"Then why won't you tell me what you talked about?"

"Because we didn't talk about anything *special*. We just talked."

"I'm not going to get on that boat or whatever it is . . . I'm really not, Tom."

"Then you're just stupid," he said, louder than he wanted to. "Look, Sharon, if she was kidnapping us, would she wake us up and let us get out? Wouldn't she just leave us sleeping?"

"I don't know."

Suddenly Aunt Eve was standing next to them. "All right, children, the island is waiting."

Sharon stood by herself as Aunt Eve and Tom started slowly off toward the end of the dock. Then, caught by feelings of fear and loneliness, she hurried to follow them. Their footsteps sounded loud in her ears as they got close to the ramp. Now Tom seemed to have a moment of hesitation, and stopped.

"Decided to stay on shore?" Aunt Eve asked, next to him.

With her gentle question in his ears, he started down, Sharon following, both of them holding on to a rope handrail which ran along one side of the ramp. At the bottom was a barge almost as wide as it was long. Their hearts were pounding. For both of them now it had become like the kind of dream in which you keep doing something even though your mind is yelling at you to stop. A few more steps, and they were on the barge.

They had left a world behind.

The barge shook hard, churning away from the dock. It shook and it creaked. In less than half a minute they couldn't see the dock behind them any more. Then, with Aunt Eve, they walked slowly forward to the low wall which ran across the front of the barge and stood, Sharon in the middle, looking ahead at nothing, hearing and smelling the salt water. Tom wondered how whoever was running the barge could know what direction to go in, with nothing but blackness and the stars around, and decided that he was probably used to making night trips.

"How long will it take, Aunt Eve?"

"That depends on the tide and the current and the wind, Tom."

"Oh. How late is it now?"

"It's past midnight. Don't worry, the captain is used to making this trip. We'll get there safely."

He wished his watch, which had a luminous dial, wasn't broken and lying in his top bureau drawer at home under his socks. He felt cold, close to shivering. The wind was coming almost straight into their faces, and every so often a dose of water blew over them. He wanted nothing more now than to get back into the car and go back to sleep.

"Are you cold?" he asked Sharon. "You want to get back into the car and go back to sleep?"

"You can go back in the car if you want to, I'll be all right."

"No, I'm O.K.," he said, determined that he'd stand it as long as she did.

Sharon looked over to him standing there in his black raincoat and hat, making a darker figure against the dark sky, and felt glad he was with her, in spite of her anger at him. Two summers before, when he had been away at camp, he had sent her a long letter in which he had written, twice, "I miss you." At the end of the letter he had said, "I couldn't like you more even if you were my brother and a boy." She still had that letter, somewhere, though she couldn't remember exactly where, which was especially too bad because it was the only letter he wrote her the whole month he was at camp.

She couldn't see his face clearly, but she didn't have to. She knew it well. It was a friendly face, and looking at it always made her feel better about all the other faces in the world. An alert face, with a narrow nose and a mouth that was always ready to laugh at funny things but never at cruel things. An attractive face, but more than that, and better than that, an honest and hopeful face.

She looked ahead again and tried to imagine what the island would be like. She gave it a name, "Senior Citizens' Island." She could see in her mind a crowd of old men and old women rolling around on the beach in wheelchairs, and getting stuck deep in the sand with no one anywhere young enough or strong enough to pull them out. She could see the beach, littered with empty, tilting wheelchairs, from which bony old men and women were crawling painfully away while the tide crept up after them, wetting their twisted yellow feet. Even Aunt Eve, the moment she touched the island, would probably get right into a wheelchair and roll away in it at high speed. Then Sharon imagined two wheelchairs stuck deep in the sand waiting for her and Tom and surrounded by old people who stared and smiled at them through loose teeth.

She shivered, moved a few inches closer to Tom,

and began imagining something happier. She could see the two of them exploring the island together, maybe finding the frame of an old whaleboat and stealing souvenirs from it to put away with their other treasures when they got back home.

When they got back home.

When would that be?

"Is it much longer, Aunt Eve?" Tom asked, as if he understood what Sharon wanted to know.

"Quite a while. Come on, both of you, I'll bed you down on the back seat again."

Aunt Eve turned and walked back to the car. The picture of her sitting in a wheelchair was still somewhere in Sharon's mind, so she was surprised to see her walking so easily. She followed along, suddenly very tired. In a few minutes they were both asleep in the car, and Aunt Eve and the captain, whose name was Homer Patience, were sitting alone together in the little pilot room in the stern of the barge, looking ahead and saying nothing.

iv

The Island Comes to Tea

"What time was it when we got here?"

"I don't know."

"We'll have to ask her."

Between mouthfuls of scrambled eggs, sticky buns, bacon, and toast with sweet orange marmalade, Tom and Sharon talked. It was well past noon, and the sun was bright. The worries and fears of Friday night were gone. In their place was the smell of the sea. Had they been kidnapped? What a question to ask, when the front door was half open to the breeze, and Aunt Eve was in the kitchen baking cookies.

The house in which they were eating and talking was old and smelled good. There was a gray slate roof on top, a dark red brick chimney at one end, and a big white door with a brass knocker in the middle. It was shingled with cedar, and rosebushes grew under the front windows. To the left as you came in the door was the living room. To the right, through double doors that were always open, was the dining room. In back there was a big kitchen. Up the wide center staircase and to the left were two bedrooms. To the right was a larger bedroom, which was Aunt Eve's, and a bathroom.

There were lots of windows, so the house was full of light all day long. At night the downstairs draperies were drawn, making it wonderfully cozy, especially when there was a fire in the fireplace (which there almost always was, once Tom took the job of setting and tending it). There were no dark portraits of long-dead ancestors, painted by long-dead painters, anywhere in the house. No bearded grandfather peered down from his frame over the fireplace, no big-eyed grandmother stared along the hall, no ancient cousin twice removed, dressed like a retired admiral on his way to a public funeral, glared wall-eyed over the top of the staircase. Instead, there were three big paintings of the sea—one over the living-room fireplace, one in the upstairs hall, and one in Tom's bedroom.

It was a good house.

After breakfast, Aunt Eve suggested that they take a walk into the village and look around. "There's not a lot to see, but you can see what there is, and it'll help you feel more at home. You just turn right in front of the house and walk straight ahead. . . . I need you back by mid-afternoon. The islanders are coming to tea and want to meet you."

"Can we help you wash the dishes?" Sharon asked, because she thought she ought to.

"No, thank you," Aunt Eve said, "but this afternoon, when we have to clean up after forty-seven tea guests, you can both help."

"Sharon'll wash and I'll dry," Tom said, on his way out the front door.

They walked out of the house and down the front path and turned right, along the cobbled road, which was lined with trees. The air smelled wonderful. In no time they were in the middle of the village.

"Look, Tom, there aren't any hands on that clock." Sharon was pointing to the steeple of a big white building that stood on Main Street facing down Harbor Road. Over the front door, a white sign with black lettering said MEETING HOUSE, and near the top of the steeple was a clock face with no hands. They walked around the building. On each side of the steeple, north, south, east, and west, there was a clock face with no hands.

"Funny," Tom said when they had gotten all the way around. He shrugged, and then he smiled.

"Maybe they just don't care what time it is."

They climbed the steps which led up to the porch of the Meeting House, turned around, and gazed over the town. They saw some houses, a movie theater called "The Jewel," a drugstore, the office of *The Weekly Islander*, and a general store.

"That must be where people get their groceries," Sharon said.

"Must be. You want to go look inside?" Tom asked her.

"No. Not today."

So far they hadn't seen any people. Even the general store was deserted, though its door was wide open and the red and white striped awning was out over the sidewalk. "Maybe they're all just sitting around at home biting their fingernails and getting ready for the big tea party," Tom said. "It's probably the biggest party they've had here for years."

They walked down Harbor Road to the dock. Aunt Eve's blue Chevrolet was still sitting on the deck of the barge, which was tied fore and aft to the heavy pilings.

"You know, I started to wonder last night too if maybe we weren't being kidnapped," Tom said quietly as they stood looking down at the barge. "It seems silly, now."

Sharon didn't say anything.

After a while they went back to Aunt Eve's house. "Is it almost time, Aunt Eve?" Tom shouted when he opened the door.

"You have lots of time to change before anyone comes," she called from the kitchen. "Don't forget to wash. You'll find things to wear in your rooms."

They ran upstairs. Sharon went into her room and Tom into his. He flopped down on his bed to rest and think for a minute. He had just smoothed out the bedspread under his stomach when Sharon came in with a funny expression on her face.

"I want to show you something."

"What?"

"I just want to show you something." She turned and walked out. Tom followed her. She walked into her room, with Tom right behind her, and over to her closet. It was full of beautiful clothes.

"Look," Sharon said.

"That's a lot of dresses," Tom said. He didn't sound impressed.

"It's not all dresses," Sharon said. "It's other things, jumpers and suits and blouses, and look at all those shoes." There were six pairs. "I hope they don't fit me," she said firmly.

"Why not?"

"I don't know. I just hope they don't fit me. I hope that none of these things fit me."

"She'd just go and buy you some more things," Tom said.

"I know," she said.

He shrugged his shoulders and started out. "We'd better get dressed."

"But at least maybe I'd be with her when she did

it," Sharon said, still staring at the clothes. "They wouldn't just be hanging here, gotten when I didn't know it."

Tom didn't answer. He was already in the bathroom. She was left alone, staring at her gallery of cottons and silks and soft, soft wools.

She still hoped that nothing would fit, but at the same time she was sure that everything would, so since they were in her room anyway, and since she was expected to come down to tea with some kind of something on, and since there was nothing else to do, she decided to put on the most grownup-looking thing in the closet, a green silk dress with a narrow round collar with black embroidery on it. She took the dress out, felt it, and after washing herself and getting into a slip, she put it on. When she saw herself in the mirror, she thought she looked almost perfect—young but at the same time very grown up. Wiser. She glanced back into the crowded closet and suddenly she was delighted to know that everything in it would probably fit her perfectly.

Aunt Eve's voice came from downstairs. "Tom? Are you and Sharon ready? Our guests are here." They were ready, so they walked downstairs in a dignified way, feeling just the slightest bit nervous. Stepping slowly into the living room, they found a dozen old people staring back at them.

"Tom, Sharon, I want to present some of my friends to you." She said this as if it were a speech in a school play. Then she led them around. The gentle-men stood for Sharon as she came by, and everyone shook Tom's hand. It really wasn't so bad at all, and Aunt Eve got them through the introductions very quickly.

She didn't act as if any one of the guests was especially important, but it was clear from the way he looked, and the way he stood, that Mr. Hill, the druggist, was special. He was tall, with white hair, about fifty-five or sixty years old, and owned the house across the road.

"He's about as young as Aunt Eve," Sharon thought, glancing at him for the third time. She liked his face.

Soon each guest was sitting in a quiet and refined posture while Aunt Eve went around with tea. Sharon followed her with a silver tray of hot biscuits and napkins, and Tom came after with sugar, lemon, and milk. After the tea had been passed, and Sharon had gone around a second time with the biscuits, there was some talk. Once it got started, people just talked at random. Nobody listened to anybody.

The first talk came out of Mrs. Kilmer, an old lady who sat with her tea and five biscuits in a far corner of the room. After wiping her mouth carefully with her napkin, she said in a very clear and rather musical voice: "The boy's got a good head. I like the shape of his head. It will be nice to have a head like that here. Turn and let me see your profile, sonny . . . You do have a well-shaped head." She fell silent and placed a whole biscuit in her mouth. She had done her bit toward the success of the party, and now it was someone else's turn.

"Lovely weather today." These words came from Mrs. Balfour, a woman of about fifty, dressed in a pink linen suit, who was sitting on the piano bench with her pocketbook between her knees. No one answered her, so she decided she would construct another sentence and push it into the room. She looked straight at Tom. "My brother—he's not here now, you know, he's coming with group 3—my brother says that it's going to be very dry this summer, especially in July."

Everyone in the room took this prediction as if it hadn't been made.

"Well, tell me, you two, how do you like our island?" This was said by a fat gentleman named Smith. Tom and Sharon answered that they liked the island very much.

"Enough to stay forever?" Mr. Smith asked. For a moment no one in the room moved or breathed, and then someone asked Mr. Smith how his potato plants were coming along, and he answered that his tomato plants had gotten a good start but that he would need more rain for his squash. As he said this, he frowned at Mrs. Balfour as if she, or at least her brother, were to blame for the dry weather to come.

"My brother hasn't said anything about the weather, but then he never does," another lady said. Then all at once there was a lot of talk everywhere, and lots of compliments given to Tom and Sharon on how nicely they looked, stood, dressed, walked, sat, spoke, smiled, and deported themselves. The compliments went on and on. It was awful. Tom and Sharon kept trying to smile and at the same time look modest. They had never been so uncomfortable with a group of adults in their lives. Fortunately, the guests got up to leave right after they had had their tea and emptied the biscuit plates.

"You certainly do deport yourselves well," Mrs. Kilmer said to Tom as she shook his right hand with her right hand and felt his head with her left. The tea guests, full of smiles and biscuits, moved in a slow, orderly line out the front door, ladies first, with many little bows and handshakings. Sharon even found herself making two or three curtsies, or near-curtsies. "Lovely deportment, lovely deportment."

The last to leave was Mr. Hill, who invited them to come to his drugstore "anytime Sunday afternoon." They thanked him for his invitation and said they'd come. When everyone was gone, Aunt Eve shut the door and turned and looked at them. "You behaved like royalty," she said, and somehow her compliment sounded different from all the compliments that had echoed among the teacups. It was pure praise, the kind their father sometimes read to them out of the Book of Psalms.

Aunt Eve walked toward the kitchen. "Only three more groups and we're done, children."

Three more tea parties, each one exactly like the

last. But in none of the three did they meet anyone with the dignity and self-possession of Mr. Hill. They saw one familiar face, that of Homer Patience, whom they remembered vaguely from the night before. He looked strange with a necktie on. And they met Mr. Eliot, the editor of *The Weekly Islander*. He came with tea group 4 and immediately backed the children into a corner to "interview" them. All of his questions started with the same phrase, "May I say that . . . ?" and so all of his questions, or almost all of them anyway, could be answered with a simple yes or no.

"May I say that you enjoyed your trip here?"

"Yes."

"May I say that you are glad to be here?"

"Yes."

"May I say that you have long looked forward to coming here?"

"Yes."

"May I say that you'll be staying with your aunt?"

"Yes."

"May I say that all of us should expect to see you both wandering happily here and there over our island in the company of adult companions, exploring its many interesting sights and wondering at its scenic magnificence, while at the same time acquiring the characteristics of speech, dress, and outlook which make this idyllic paradise in the midst of the sea the miracle of balance and peace that it is?"

They didn't answer.

He waited silently. Finally, they both said yes, almost together, just so he'd stop staring at them. He had a lot more yes-or-no questions, and then, suddenly, he was through. He stepped one step back. He smiled.

"You'll be able to read the interview in our Sunday edition. I know you'll like it."

Then his photographer, Mr. Rice, took a picture of them. His flashbulb popped so fast that they had no time to get their faces ready. Mr. Rice gulped a quick "thank you" and faded away.

After the last guest had gone, Aunt Eve, Tom, and Sharon—all wearing big aprons—did the dishes. Then Tom and Sharon changed and went into the pine woods behind Mr. Hill's house to hunt for the-world's-most-perfect-pine-cone. The woods refreshed and renewed them. The ground was covered with a thick layer of pine needles, which made the walking soft and almost completely silent. The smell in the air wasn't so much piney as it was clean, and though the woods had a feeling of mystery about them, it wasn't a scary mystery.

After tramping around for a while, they decided to find two pine cones, the-world's-most-perfect-pine-cone and the-world's-second-most-perfect-pine-cone. That way each of them would have a souvenir. They'd let Aunt Eve decide which one would get which pine cone. They picked up a lot of cones, but by the time they started back to Aunt Eve's they had thrown them all away because none of them was quite perfect enough. "We've got lots of time to hunt pine cones," Tom said.

"How long are we going to be here?" Sharon asked.

"I don't know. If you want to know, why don't you ask Aunt Eve?"

"That wouldn't be nice," Sharon said. "She'd think I didn't like it here. Maybe you could ask her later."

"Why me?"

"Because you're older."

"But I don't care how long we stay. I like it here. I don't care if we stay here forever."

Sharon didn't say anything, and for a while they just walked on quietly through the woods. Then she said, "Well, I do."

"Do what?"

"Care whether we stay here forever or not."

"I was only fooling. I didn't mean that I'd really like to stay forever."

"We have to remember," Sharon said as if she hadn't heard him, "that this isn't home. I just think we have to remember that."

"We'll remember," Tom said, "don't worry."

"Then will you ask her for me sometime? I don't mean right today, but sometime?"

"Sure."

At that she began to run back toward Aunt Eve's house, and they ran side by side until they came to her front door.

v 🌿🌿🌿

A Question, an Answer

Dinner was a big fruit salad, iced coffee, and chocolate cake. Just before the cake, Tom said, "I think I'll write Dad and Mom a letter tonight. Don't you think that's a good idea, Aunt Eve?"

"No."

Her pure no was so unexpected, so unbelievable, that for a moment it didn't get through to him. "You don't think it would be a good idea?"

"No."

Tom didn't know what to say. He almost started whistling, just to fill the silence. Then Aunt Eve changed the subject. "Do your mother and father ever read to you at night before you go to bed?"

"Sometimes," Tom answered. "They used to do it a lot." She passed Tom another piece of cake. Suddenly he wasn't hungry any more, but he took it and started eating anyway.

"Do you know *The Swiss Family Robinson?*" she asked. Tom did. At least he had seen a movie of it. "No, I don't," he said.

"Well, we'll start reading it tonight then."

Since Aunt Eve's "no," Sharon hadn't put any food in her mouth. Aunt Eve looked over to her. "You'll have a chance to write home soon," she said. "Not now, but soon."

A Novel, Some Letters

The Swiss Family Robinson is a fantastic story about four children who are shipwrecked on an island with their parents and have to live there for ten years with nothing to help them but cleverness, optimism, and a few tools that are washed ashore with them. It's a marvelous story which couldn't possibly have happened the way it's written, but you believe it anyway all the time you're reading it.

That night Aunt Eve began reading it aloud in

front of the fire. The first chapter was boring. Half-way through the second chapter it began to get interesting. Sharon sat trying not to listen, but by the middle of the third chapter she was completely hooked, and so was Tom. When Chapter 3 was over, Aunt Eve closed the book. Neither Tom nor Sharon asked her to read on.

In the far end of the living room, the part toward the back of the house, there were bookshelves and a small desk with a lot of books and papers on it. Aunt Eve turned her head toward that part of the room. "You two might be interested in some of my books. You're welcome to rummage around among them any time." She turned toward Tom. "While I think of it, there are some tools in the basement, and a good deal of lumber. Not enough to build a boat, but you could make almost anything else, if you have the patience. Have you?"

"I don't know."

"You probably haven't, but you're capable of it. You only need the chance to develop it."

Tom took a deep breath. "Can we write letters at the desk?"

Aunt Eve didn't look a bit surprised. Tom wasn't sure, but she might even have had a slight smile on her face for a moment before she answered him. "For practice in spelling and composition, you may write all the letters you want, but don't expect me to mail them for you."

Tom said no more. He looked around for a clock. He had already done that five or six times before, and now he realized again that there were no clocks anywhere.

Aunt Eve stood up.

"It's time for me to go to bed." She started toward the door, and when she got there she turned around and looked toward Sharon. "As long as we're together on this island I'll never knowingly tell you a lie or break a promise. You can be sure that my 'yes' will mean yes, and my 'no' will mean no. And if I change my mind about something, I'll let you know right away. I said I would allow you to write home soon, and I meant it. Turn off the lights before you come upstairs, will you please? Except for the porch light. I always leave that on."

"What did she say that about telling the truth for?" Tom asked after they heard her shut the bathroom door upstairs.

"I believe her," Sharon said, still staring at the spot where she had last seen Aunt Eve. "Do you?"

"Sure."

She looked over to him. "You shouldn't just say 'sure' like that. How do you know she wouldn't lie to us?"

"I don't know," Tom said. "The same way you know, I guess." There was a puzzled look on his face now. "How do *you* know she wouldn't?"

"Because of the way she looked at me. She looked

at me in a different way, as if I weren't a child any more. I think she might do terrible things. She might even do terrible things to us. But she wouldn't lie to us, not now that she's got us here."

"You really think she might do terrible things to us?" Tom was more curious than frightened.

"How should I know? . . . I don't think so, but who knows?" She got up and went to the far corner of the room. "I wonder what kind of books she has here."

Tom came over, and the two of them started to look at the shelves of books without really seeing any of them . . . just to have something to do. Then Tom noticed a loose-leaf notebook, with TOM written on the front of it, lying on the desk. He opened it slowly. On the first page was his name, his birth date, his parents' names, his place of birth, his birth weight, and a lot of other official information like that.

He began turning the pages, stopping to read here and there. Every page had a letter Scotch-taped to it and every letter began with *Dear Eve,* and ended with, *As ever, J.H.* Someone had been watching him —spying on him—from time to time almost since the day he was born, and reporting to Aunt Eve in letters. Sharon began watching over his shoulder. He usually didn't like to have anyone doing that, but this time he was too interested in what he was reading to care. He stopped at a letter that had been written the previous February 3, his birthday:

Dear Eve,

Today is Tom's birthday.

This afternoon he went with a group of friends to the skating rink in Central Park. His ice-skating skill continues to improve, though to-day he had some difficulty at first because of new ice skates with long runners.

After he had skated with his friends for a while, he began to help a younger boy who was just learning. He went on helping the boy and talking to him until about 5:30. Then he left the boy and skated again with his friends until he left the rink with them and went home.

The letter went on talking about his health, his friends, and how he was doing in school, and ended, "If we want him, this is the year to get him. As ever, J.H."

Tom remembered February 3. He remembered his birthday breakfast—pancakes and sausages—and his new skates on the table next to his plate. His father had given him a waterproof watch, and that night his mother sat on the end of his bed and told him again the story of what had happened the day he was born. Tom never got tired of hearing that story. Suddenly, with the memory of that day ever so clear in his mind, he wanted to go home. He wanted his mother to tuck him in and kiss him good night. He wanted to see his father's raincoat hanging in the hall again—it was almost always there, even on rainy days. He wanted to be in his own room with his own old things.

He closed the book, and because he was afraid that he might cry he went to the window, pushed the draperies apart, and stared out into the dark. Oh, to be home, to be settled in bed, maybe reading a story he'd already read from a book he already knew. To go to sleep and to wake up with all the things he knew and loved. To hear his mother's voice.

Even to be sick, as long as he was sick at home.

He stood at the window quite a while, watching the dim street and the trees whose leaves shivered from time to time in a light breeze. Slowly the feeling of being about to cry started to go away. He turned around and saw Sharon standing at the desk reading. It made him mad, seeing her reading away like that as if he'd said it was all right for her to do it.

"Who said you could read my letters?"

He walked over to the desk and shut the notebook. She looked up at him. Now she was angry. "What did you do that for? It isn't your book, it's mine." She pointed to her name on the cover. "I didn't even look at yours. I was only reading the first page, anyway. You ought to look at things before you get mad."

"Oh." He suddenly felt awful. "I'm sorry, Sharon. Really."

She didn't open her book up again. The two looseleaf books lay beside each other on the desk. Tom looked at her.

"Let's go to bed. There's nothing to do down here."

"Don't go ahead of me. Let's go together."

"You want to bring anything with you?"

She looked around idly. "I don't think so."

Tom made sure the screen was in front of the fireplace, in which a tiny flame was still curling around the end of a log. Then he went to the master switch next to the entrance to the living room and turned off all the lights. Both of them stood for a moment watching the fire play behind the screen across the room, and then they went into the hall.

"I wish I knew what time it was," Tom said as they started up the stairs. "How do you suppose these people know when to do things?"

She followed him into his room and sat down on the end of his bed and looked as if she were going to cry.

They started to talk.

First they talked about the barge, and then about the dock, and then about the village, and then about the houses on Main Street, and then about the tea parties, and then about Aunt Eve. When they got to her, they first talked about the money she used to send them, and then about how little she looked like her photographs, and then, finally, about why she had brought them here.

"What if you were trying to kidnap somebody . . ." Tom began, but he never finished his sentence because the idea of Aunt Eve as a kidnapper still seemed ridiculous. "No, she's too nice. Besides, she doesn't need the money anyway."

"What money."

"The ransom."

"Oh . . . Why won't she let us write home, then?"

"I don't know. It doesn't make any sense. But she did say we could write later."

"Why later? Why not now?"

"I don't know. It doesn't make any sense."

"Why don't you ask her?"

"Ask her what?"

"Why we can't write now . . . whether she's kidnapped us or not."

"You can't do that, ask somebody if she's a kidnapper. I'll bet she's sent each of us a thousand dollars since we were born. Kidnappers don't send you money. And she's been nice to us, except for the part about writing home."

"You think it's all right, then? You think Mom and Dad know where we are, and everything's really all right?"

Tom thought a minute. "Probably. And even if they don't know, there's nothing we can do about it." He thought another minute. "On top of everything else, I just think she's too smart to be a crook."

"She is too smart to get caught, anyway," Sharon said.

Outside, crickets chirped. Somewhere a screen door slammed. Sharon yawned and stretched. "It must be late, I think I'll go to bed." Tom looked up. "And we haven't even got any clocks around here to tell the time with," he said. Sharon straightened out her legs and stood up. "I'll see you in the morning," she said, and went out of the room. Then she came back to the door. "I wish we knew," she whispered. "I just wish we *knew*."

And then she went to bed.

A minute or so later, lying alone in the dark, with no sound anywhere but the sound of the crickets, Sharon tried to figure her feelings out. She was nervous, and she was afraid, and she knew it, but not so nervous or so afraid that she couldn't control herself. She wasn't shaking, she wasn't sweating, she wasn't even biting her fingernails. That was good. It was like finding out in a gym test that you're stronger than you thought you were. She relaxed, a little, turned over on her side, and closed her eyes.

Meanwhile, Tom lay in his bed thinking about the two books of letters downstairs on the desk. He hoped that they'd still be there in the morning. He decided he'd offer a straight trade with Sharon. He'd let her read the letters about him, if she let him read the letters about her.

That seemed fair.

He grew sleepier, and his mind drifted back to *The Swiss Family Robinson*. His last thoughts before going to sleep were about the four brave Robinson children, far away from help, in the middle of the ocean.

❦❦ *vii* ❧❧❧

"A Fate Worse than Death"

The next morning Aunt Eve got them up early. Tom guessed that it was around six when they were half-way through breakfast. "I'm going away for a few days, children," Aunt Eve said. "I expect to be back Wednesday. While I'm gone you can have at least one meal a day with Mr. Hill across the street. He's not as good a cook as I am, but he makes wonderful soups." She poured herself some more coffee.

"Mr. Simpson gives a lecture at the Meeting House

every Sunday, and you may want to go and listen to him this morning. He's honest, but he's also stupid. If you go, you and Mr. Hill will be the only ones there, and you'll probably be bored and uncomfortable, but hearing Mr. Simpson, and talking with Mr. Hill about him, may help you understand the island better."

"We'll have to change into different clothes if we go," Sharon said, looking down at her dungarees and sweat shirt.

"No, you won't," Aunt Eve said. "In fact, Mr. Simpson would be especially pleased to have you come to his lecture dressed just as you are." She looked over to them. "Mr. Hill will probably invite you to go for a picnic with him tomorrow. Please feel free to say no. He won't be offended at all if you do. However, you really ought to go with him, because he knows the island better than anyone else, and because he's a gentleman. Do you know any gentlemen, Tom?"

"My father."

"Yes, I dare say you're right. And even if you're wrong, it's a gentlemanly answer. Will you pass the toast, please?"

He passed the toast. "Where are you going?"

"To New York. While I'm gone, you're free to use anything in the house. Just don't throw anything away. And do be careful if you go exploring on the south side of the island. It's dangerous footing in some places there, especially on the big rocks near the shore. They get as slippery as oil when they're wet."

She put down the knife with which she was buttering her toast, and spoke more slowly. "I won't be foolish and tell you to be good while I'm gone. I've put you in a very difficult position here, and I know you'll be as good as you can be under the circumstances, and nobody can ask for more than that."

"What are you going to do in New York?" Sharon asked.

"Talk to your parents, go to the Metropolitan Museum of Art, and, if I have time, visit the seals in Central Park Zoo."

Sharon got in her mind a picture of Aunt Eve standing by the seal pool. She was carrying a big pocketbook. Slowly she reached into her pocketbook and slowly she drew out a long fish, and threw it high in the air. A seal flew up and caught it.

Tom examined his empty orange-juice glass. "What do you want to talk to them about?"

"I can't tell you that yet. No, that's not so. I can tell you, but I don't choose to. I'll only tell you that I'm going to see them, and talk to them, and try to make this business a little less hard for them, and for you, and for myself. Have you had enough breakfast? . . . Good . . . Would you mind walking with me to the ferry? I'd like to talk with you some more."

At the door, Aunt Eve picked up a dark brown leather suitcase and a light brown cloth bag which was tied at the top with a leather shoestring. Tom took both of them from her and led the way out of the house. A few moments later they were walking down the road, Aunt Eve in the middle.

"Tom, answer me honestly, when you think of me, what else do you think of?"

"Money."

"Exactly," Aunt Eve said. "Money. Thank you, Tom."

"And having to write thank-you notes," Sharon said, and the three of them laughed briefly, even though Sharon hadn't meant it as a joke, and didn't want to laugh with this woman.

"You think of money," Aunt Eve said, "and the thought of having it, and getting more of it, makes you feel good. Of course, money can't make people love you, but it can help people to like you, and if it comes regularly, for a long time, it can even lead people to trust you more. That's why I sent you and your parents money so often for so long, so that when the time came for me to call you on the phone and tell you to walk out of your apartment and come away with me, you'd have less hesitation about it. I bought some of your trust, and now you feel that perhaps you've been betrayed. You have.

"So, while I'm away these few days, you can get used to the idea that your dear old Aunt Eve isn't just a rich, sweet old lady, but that she is, among other things, a kidnapper."

They turned left toward the dock and began walking a little faster because Harbor Road ran slightly downhill. When they got halfway to the dock, Aunt Eve said, "We're going to be living together for a long time, children, and the sooner you feel a need for me, the better. I've felt the need for you for at least ten years. You may never come to love me—I have no control over that—but I can help you to realize that you need me, and that's a beginning."

"Do Mom and Dad know where we are?" Tom asked. He wasn't the least bit afraid, but he was angry.

"No. By tonight they'll know that you're safe, but they don't know it yet, and even tonight I won't tell them where you are. This has been the most terrible weekend in their lives."

Tom and Sharon both imagined how their apartment must look with a dozen policemen searching it. But neither of them could imagine, though they both tried hard, how their parents' faces looked.

Aunt Eve spoke again, "Don't worry yourselves about escaping while I'm gone, because there isn't any escape, and I don't want you to get hurt trying to find one. Please understand, children, you have been well kidnapped."

They arrived at the dock. The barge was waiting. Homer Patience was there, but he stood back to give Aunt Eve a chance to say goodbye.

"One day, sooner than you think, you'll be staying on this island because you want to."

"Does that mean you're not going to try to get ransom for us?" Tom asked.

"Tom, the last thing I need from the world is money. And the first thing I need, the first thing all of us here need, is Tom and Sharon Inlander. We plan to keep you."

After the barge had pulled slowly away, Tom and Sharon sat on the edge of the dock, their feet dangling over the water, watching it as it got smaller and smaller. It took a long time for it to go out of sight. Tom got up. "Come on," he said, and started running back up Harbor Road. At Main Street he turned left, away from Aunt Eve's house, and kept running. After a hundred feet or so, Main Street went right and began climbing uphill. Three hundred feet farther on, it narrowed and became a path. Tom stopped where the path reached the edge of the woods, and waited for Sharon. A few seconds after she had reached him, he asked her if she'd caught her breath yet.

"One minute," she said. Tom tried to be patient and wait, and Sharon tried to hurry up and catch her breath, and before she had done it she said "O.K.," and they started running again. The path did a lot of twisting through the trees, and then it came out into the open just below the top of the hill. They stopped.

To the west—they knew it was west because the sun was behind them—they could see the coast of Maine very clearly. "A good swimmer could swim there," Tom said. Sharon shook her head. "It looks an awful long way to me. Neither of us could ever make it." They turned and ran on until they got to the very top of the hill. There they saw a big circle of stones. Inside the circle was a jumble of charred logs and branches, and hanging by a string from one long black branch was an envelope. Tom pulled it off and opened it up. The note inside said,

Dear Tom and Sharon,

Every few days for the past five summers I've had someone come up here and make a big smoky fire, sometimes during the day and sometimes at night. At first the Forest Rangers on the mainland had the Coast Guard investigate, but now they don't bother any more.

I'm sorry you have to be disappointed this way. It was a good idea.

You're probably too angry to be hungry or thirsty, but if you aren't, there's a stone jug of water, two cups, and a tin box of cookies next to the orange-colored stone on the far side of the circle. Again, I'm sorry you're disappointed, but you wouldn't want to be kidnapped by too much of an amateur, would you? See you Wednesday.

Love,
Aunt Eve

Tom didn't say a word. He had never felt so disappointed and trapped in his life. He let the letter go as if it were covered with poison. It fluttered away in the breeze. Then he walked around the circle to the orange-colored stone, picked up the round tin box next to it, and pulled the lid off. It was full of big, dark brown cookies. He took one out and threw it at a bush halfway down the bare part of the hill. It missed. He took another cookie, and missed again.

"You want a try?" he said to Sharon. She shook her head. So he sat down and, one by one, threw the cookies at the bush, which was downhill but quite far away. Then he closed the tin and threw it. Then he threw the cups, which were made of pottery, and then he tried to throw the jug, and almost dropped it on his foot.

Out of twenty cookies, he had hit the bush four times. He had missed with both cups, but the tin had made a perfect hit.

He got up and went over to Sharon, who was sitting on the grass. "I hate her," she said. "I just hate her. What right has she got?" She clenched her teeth. She was close to crying. Then, slowly, she got up and started back down the hill, trying to think of ways to embarrass Aunt Eve and give her pain. Tom came beside her and pretty soon they were walking back down Harbor Road again. As she got closer to the dock, a picture came into her mind of all the people on the island crowded together into a room with white walls. In the middle, on a high stool, sat

Aunt Eve deciding whom she was going to bother with. Most of the people around the room looked frightened and hateful. A few, like Mr. Hill, looked calm, almost bored. Aunt Eve's gaze took everybody in. Sharon studied her face.

"The only ones she cares for," Sharon said, not looking at Tom, "are the ones who aren't afraid of her, like Mr. Hill. She likes him more than any of them. . . . It would be terrible if we ever got really scared of her."

"Why?" Tom asked.

"I don't know," Sharon said. All of a sudden a feeling of complete helplessness, almost paralysis, overcame her. "Why ask me? You're the one who ought to know about everything. You're older. You're the one who talked to her on the phone in the first place, anyway, and said everything was all right. . . . You're the one who got us here."

By now they were at the end of the dock. They stood and looked at the water and thought about home. After a while the bell in the Meeting House steeple began to ring. At first they didn't notice it because the seagulls were making a lot of noise, but after a while they heard it.

"Let's go to church," Tom said.

"You never want to go to church at home," Sharon answered quickly.

"What do you mean?"

"I mean you never want to go to church when you're home, that's all, so I was just wondering why you want to go to church now all of a sudden. Anyway, it's not a church. It's a meeting house."

Tom looked straight at her. "Look, Sharon, if you want to argue about something important, O.K., we'll sit down and argue about it, but let's not argue about silly things like how often I feel like going to church." What Tom said sounded so much like the kind of thing their father sometimes said to their mother that they were both deeply surprised. They stared at each other. Then Sharon turned around, and they walked silently and slowly up Harbor Road to the Meeting House.

The door was wide open. They went inside and sat down near the back, trying not to move so their bench wouldn't squeak. Mr. Hill was sitting in the second pew from the front on the left side, and they watched the back of his head until Mr. Simpson— short, fat, and bald-headed—walked with dignity down the center aisle. He wore the same suit he had worn to tea the day before, and he didn't seem to notice, or care, whether there were other people in the building or not.

"The question which we will consider during the next seventeen Sundays," he said when he got to the pulpit, "is this: What does the word *truth* mean? The philosopher, Spinoza, defines the *truth* in seven distinct ways. . . ."

Mr. Simpson went on, and on, and on, and on, and on, and on. And then he went on some more. And then he went on, and went on. A fly ran back and

forth on the seat between Tom and Sharon. A breeze
blew in through the door. The fly flew away. After
a long time, he came back. In a rack in front of them
there were cards for visitors to fill out, and a short
pencil. After they had been sitting still nearly forever, Sharon took one of the cards and wrote on the
back of it, "There *are* fates worse than death," and
passed it over to Tom.

He looked down at the note and nodded. There
were fates worse than death, and one of them was
having to listen to an eternal lecture. Finally, after
reading pages and pages of text, Mr. Simpson
stopped, smiled, said, "May we all be kept from
the slippery rocks so that we may gather here again
next Sunday," and walked briskly up the aisle, wiping
his forehead with a handkerchief. As he went by,
Tom turned his head and saw from Sharon's face
that she had been crying. He pretended not to
notice.

They sat still until Mr. Hill had passed their pew,
so that they wouldn't have to be the first ones out
the door. He stopped on the broad top step and shook
Mr. Simpson's hand. "There were some interesting
things in your lecture this morning, Mr. Simpson.
Thank you for being so good as to deliver it."

"Thank you very kindly, I'm sure, Mr. Hill," Mr.
Simpson said modestly, his round face still shiny
with perspiration. He wiped it with his handkerchief
again, looked at Tom and Sharon, shook their hands,

thanked them for coming, and invited them to come every Sunday.

"Of course, you may not be able to understand everything, but such things are nevertheless good for your intellectual development, all things considered, one way and another, don't you think?"

Tom and Sharon smiled and nodded. Mr. Simpson smiled back. "I hope you'll excuse me now?"

"Of course," Mr. Hill said.

Mr. Simpson nodded to each of them in turn and stepped back into the building like a happy jack-in-the-box.

Tom and Sharon gazed along Harbor Road and out onto the ocean. It looked gray, and there were heavy gray clouds over it. The afternoon would be rainy. With no sun and no clocks they couldn't tell whether it was noon or not, but they knew it was near noon because they were hungry.

"Let's have lunch," Mr. Hill said, and the three of them went down the steps and started along Main Street toward his house.

"I was surprised to hear you come into the Meeting House this morning. I didn't expect you."

"How did you know it was us?" Tom asked.

"Because no one else ever comes except your Aunt Eve, and she was away, so it had to be you."

"Does Aunt Eve come every week?" Sharon asked.

"Every week," he answered.

"Why?" Tom asked.

"Because she admires people of good will, even when they're stupid."

"He seems like an awfully nice old man," Sharon said. She was sorry right away for having used the word "old." A gusty, chilly wind began to blow, and the sky was getting grayer every minute.

"You're right, Sharon," Mr. Hill said after a minute or so. "We're all of us old, and dull, and useless; but maybe we won't always be useless."

When they got to his house, he led the way around it so that they entered through the back door. A light fog had settled, giving his garden a soft, dreamy look. When Tom and Sharon were inside and sitting at the kitchen table, he began again to talk about Mr. Simpson.

"He's an interesting man. I don't know whether either of you tried to understand him this morning, but if you did I'm sure it must have been discouraging, because he was talking pure nonsense. The funny thing about him is that the ideas he turns into nonsense are always important ideas, good ideas." Mr. Hill opened the refrigerator and stood with his hand on the door. "He's thoroughly stupid, but he always knows, instinctively, what's important. Remarkable, isn't it?" He looked in the refrigerator. "He's like a cook who always uses the best ingredients, and always ends up with something you can't eat." He took a pitcher of milk out and set it on the table. "Maybe one reason I'm glad he doesn't get any smarter is that I like to feel that some things just never change."

Both Tom and Sharon silently agreed with Mr. Hill that there was something special about a man like Mr. Simpson, but they weren't quite ready to admire his special kind of specialness.

"Doesn't anybody else do anything there?" Sharon asked.

"Nobody," Mr. Hill said as he poured a lot of things together into a pot on the stove. "That's really his building. He's got the only key."

"You mean he owns it?" Tom asked.

"In the sense that a man owns what he uses and nobody else wants."

"How long has he been making speeches there?"

"Ever since he retired and came to live here. He used to be a fireman in Columbus, Ohio. He saved the lives of five children once, after everyone else had given them up for dead. Another time, trying to save a youngster, he had most of the skin on his back burned off." Mr. Hill stirred the soup, which was now beginning to bubble around the edges.

Sharon began to smell the soup and realized how hungry she was. Mr. Hill took the soup off the stove, put it in bowls, poured them some milk, put some bread and butter on the table, and sat down.

"Most men spend their lives looking for a place where they can eat and drink without worrying about war and disease and misery, and most men never find it. May we always be grateful for what we've found, and been given, because it's not ours by right. Amen."

He picked up his spoon and began to eat.

"You're likable children," he said. "It's a wonder Aunt Eve didn't steal you long ago."

They laughed a small laugh. It had a slightly nervous sound.

"Let me tell you something. I've only heard laughter on this island twice in the last few years. One time was this morning, when you and your Aunt Eve were on your way down to the dock. The second time was just now. It's like food to a starving man." He paused for a moment. "Do you know what the word 'amen' means? It means 'so be it' or 'may it be so.' It's a word of hope."

They ate the rest of their meal in silence, but it was a calm, and even friendly, hopeful silence. And the soup was delicious.

❧❧ viii ❧❧❧

An Editorial

One thing Sharon liked about Mr. Hill was that he didn't keep her standing at his front door saying goodbye and making small talk until her legs got tired. When lunch was over and it was time to go, they went to the door, said goodbye, and left. No fuss, no silly talk just for the sake of talking. Two minutes after they were back at Aunt Eve's house, it began to rain and blow.

Tom made a fire.

When the middle of the afternoon came, and it was time to go downtown to Mr. Hill's drugstore, it was still pouring. They felt they ought to go, though, so they put on slickers and rain hats and some rubbers they found in the front-hall closet and splashed out. When they got to the road, they began to play tag, but Sharon slipped on a cobblestone and scraped her right knee trying to dodge a tag a minute after they began, so they had to quit. By the time they got into the middle of town, their feet squished in their shoes and water was running around under their collars and down their necks.

When they passed *The Weekly Islander* office, Sharon stopped. "What's the matter?" Tom asked, worried that it was her knee.

"I want to see what's in the newspaper about us," she said.

So did he.

A copy of the front page was taped to the inside of the office window. Rain kept running down the outside of the window, making everything but the big print hard to read. On the top of the front page, in heavy, fancy letters about an inch high, were the words *The Weekly Islander*. Under them, in half-inch-high letters, was written *A good newspaper, published each Sunday all year*. In the upper right-hand corner, in a box, were the words *Sunday Edition*, and the date. There was no price printed anywhere.

The page was divided down the middle, with a

headlined story on the right and an editorial on the left. The headline over the story said: NEWCOMERS ARRIVE.

The ferryboat *Safe Journey,* under the command of Homer Patience, Captain, brought two young strangers to our shore on Friday last. In an interview the newcomers confessed that they had enjoyed their trip here, were glad to be with us, had long looked forward to coming, and would be living permanently with their "aunt," Mrs. Eve Standish of Main Street. They stated that the Islanders should expect to see them wandering here and there over our Island in the company of adult companions, exploring its many interesting sights, and wondering at its scenic magnificence, while at the same time acquiring the characteristics of speech, dress, and outlook that make this idyllic paradise in the midst of the sea the miracle of balance and peace that it is. . . .

The story went on like this all the way to the bottom of the page. It was the silliest thing they had ever read. But they didn't feel like laughing at it. It made them angry, and sorry that they had so meekly said yes to all of Mr. Eliot's fancy questions.

The editorial on the other side of the page was in bolder print. The spaces between the lines were a little bigger, and the entire thing had a black line around it. The title of the editorial was THE WISE HOST.

It is the duty of every human being to treat his guests kindly and politely. This duty is recognized even in the world. Surely a duty which even the world recognizes *must be obeyed* on this Island. Even those who oppose the introduction of a new generation as a *dangerous change* must recognize their duty now that the outsiders have arrived.

We need have no fears for our safety *as long as we remain calm and watchful.* Surely such a paradise as ours can admit two small invaders without fear!

The editor would remind his readers of a well-known story. It is said by Ancient Authorities that the Greeks conquered Troy by leaving at its gates a Wooden Horse filled with Greek soldiers. The people of Troy, thinking that the Greeks had withdrawn and that they were safe, took the Horse into the city and celebrated the end of the Greek siege. That night, while Troy slept, the Greeks came out of the Wooden Horse's belly and destroyed the city and its people.

Let us learn a lesson from the Trojans! If they had avoided celebration, if they had spent their time watching and guarding instead of laughing and being happy, they would have been safe *even with the Greeks inside their walls!* The lesson for *our* Troy is simple. If we remain watchful and cautious, the *two possible enemies* in our midst can do us no harm. And—who knows?— we may even make two little Trojans like ourselves out of them! That is your editor's devout hope and firm expectation.

After Tom and Sharon had read it, they read it again, and then they just stood in front of the newspaper office and stared at it without really seeing it. Sharon had never used the word "outrageous" before, but now it was the only word in her mind. The editorial was outrageous. Outrageous. Outrageous. She read it a third time, slowly.

Not once on the whole front page had their names been mentioned. They were called "strangers," "newcomers," "little immigrants," "recent arrivals," "possible enemies," and, of all things, "Greeks," but never Tom and Sharon. They rather liked being called Greeks, but the rest of the names were . . . well, they were outrageous.

They stood in front of the *Islander* office for a long time, too distracted and too depressed to notice that the door which led inside was wide open.

"I don't want to go anywhere," Sharon said. "I just want to go back."

"I don't want to go, either," Tom said. "Except that maybe we should go and tell him we're not coming."

Neither of them moved. They just kept standing there in the rain. Finally Tom turned away. "Come on, let's go home." He started to run.

"Wait a minute," Sharon called after him. "My knee hurts too much for me to run." Tom waited until she caught up, and they started together for the house.

Her hurt was, in a way, a good thing for him because it gave him something else to think about besides the editorial. "Maybe we should try to get a doctor," he said as he walked extra slowly beside her.

"I don't need a doctor," she said. "I just want to get back and get dry and sit in front of the fire and not see anybody."

"You ought to wash it out with soap and water at least," Tom said, "so you don't get an infection or something." The last thing Sharon wanted was more water on her, but she didn't say it. After all, Tom was trying to help, and he was the only friend she had.

Every time they passed a house, Sharon imagined the old people inside peeking out at them from behind their curtains and hating them and maybe wishing that they were dead and buried so that their island Troy would be safe again. In spite of her knee, almost enjoying its hurting, Sharon started to walk faster.

"Be careful you don't slip again," Tom said, Sharon didn't answer. What she really wanted was for him to hold her hand. Not for long, just until they got home. But he didn't. She got ahead of him. "What are you going so slow for?" she asked, and then almost slipped again on another slippery cobblestone.

"Take it easy, we're not going anywhere special."

She didn't even slow down. Less than a minute later, they were back at the house.

When they got inside, Sharon ran limping upstairs, dripping all the way, went into the bathroom, stood in the bathtub, took all her wet clothes off, and rubbed herself down with a towel. Tom went into the kitchen and took off everything but his underwear and threw it all onto the railing of the little back porch. Then he walked into the living room in his wet underwear and concentrated on building up the fire again. Squatting down, his head cocked to one side, and an iron poker in his hand, he worked, and forgot about time.

"You better get your underwear off and some dry things on or you'll catch cold," Sharon said. She was standing behind him, barefoot but otherwise all dryly dressed, and rubbing her hair with a heavy green towel.

"How's your knee?" he asked her.

"It's O.K. I even put a Band-Aid on it." She bent it to show him it didn't hurt, and sat down cross-legged on the floor. "You better get upstairs and change too." Tom was feeling warm and didn't want to move, but he knew she was right, so after a minute more he got off the floor, went upstairs, took off his damp underwear, and threw it into the tub on top of Sharon's wet clothes. Then he dried himself off and went into his room and put on dry things. The clothes he had worn on Friday were missing, but there was a lot of new stuff to choose from, so he didn't even think about it.

He went back downstairs and sat with Sharon in front of the fire.

"These people must have figured out the secret of living forever and they're keeping it from everybody else in the world," he said, staring into the fire. Sharon was thinking the same thing, but she wanted to hear his reasons for thinking it, so she just said, "That's silly."

"I know, but that must be it anyway. Why else would everybody talk the way they do?" Tom said.

"What way?"

"You know, the things they say, calling this place 'paradise' and things like that, saying it's 'everlasting' . . . Who knows how old some of these people are? They could all be over a hundred for all we know. Maybe it's something in the water they drink. I don't know."

"It could be," Sharon said, trying to sound wise and cautious, like a judge.

"Sometimes girls can be so stupid," Tom said.

"What do you say that for?"

"I don't know," Tom said. "Forget it."

"I think I'll go find some checkers and we can play checkers. You want to?" Sharon asked, getting up and starting out of the room. "It'll be fun to play checkers in front of a fire. We never did that." By this time she was already out of the room, and a minute later she was back with a wooden checkerboard and a round can of checkers.

"Where'd you find them?"

"In my closet." They set up the board in front of the fire and played. After a few games, Sharon popped up again and went upstairs and brought down a deck of cards and they played some games of rummy. It stopped raining and a beautiful sunset appeared, but they didn't notice. Tom kept the fire burning high.

Outside, it got dark.

Somebody knocked on the door.

The knock made them feel suddenly very alone and unprotected. All the lights in the house were out because they hadn't noticed it was getting dark. They had been playing cards by firelight. They felt like leaving the lights off, hiding behind the couch, and pretending that nobody was home. They wished that Aunt Eve were back. "Well," Tom said, and his voice sounded very loud in the dark room, "I guess we better answer the door." They both started toward it at the same time, but he stopped on the way to turn on the switch for the living-room lights, so Sharon got to it first.

It was Mr. Hill. "I'm bearing gifts for two Greeks," he said, and Sharon opened the door wide. They were relieved to see him, and not just because he brought food, though that was welcome too. He had a big brown paper bag with sandwiches, a thermos bottle of hot cocoa, potato chips, sweet pickles, and a lot of fruit. Soon the three of them were eating in front of the fire and playing three-handed rummy.

"I apologize for the editorial," Mr. Hill said during their second game. "I know it must have been that, and not the rain, that kept you away this afternoon. I didn't expect Mr. Eliot to write anything like that. We expected that once we got you here everyone on the island would be as glad to have you around as we are. I hope it doesn't bother you too much. He'll change his mind, I'm sure."

"It isn't so bad," Tom said. "We kind of like the idea of being Greeks."

"He'll change his mind," Mr. Hill said again, quietly but firmly. "By the way, don't let me leave without taking your wet clothes with me."

"You don't have to do that," Sharon said.

"I'd like to. Mrs. Burns would consider it a privilege to be able to wash them for you."

"Who's Mrs. Burns?" Tom asked.

"She lives near the dock. In the house with the red shutters that sits practically on top of Harbor Road. She used to be a children's nurse. You'll be doing her a favor by letting her take care of your things."

"Does she live alone?" Sharon asked. She was beginning to think that almost everyone on the island did.

"She lives with Miss Dome, the dressmaker."

Tom carefully examined his rummy hand—it was

his turn—and wondered what Miss Dome the dress-maker might have been before she came to the island. A librarian? An apple picker? A lady wrestler? Or had she always been a dressmaker? There was a knock on the door, and he got up right away to answer it. No one was there, but when he opened the door an evelope fell into the hall. It was perfumed, and addressed *To Master Tom and Mistress Sharon Inlander*. He opened it and read the letter before he went back into the living room.

Dear Children,

  We want you to know that many people on the island are glad you are here and hope very much that you will stay forever.

       Very sincerely yours,
       Two Friendly Islanders

Tom wondered, as he carried the letter into the living room to show it to Sharon and Mr. Hill, if the "Two Friendly Islanders" who had written it were Mrs. Burns and Miss Dome.

❀❀ ix ❀❀❀

A Piece of the Past

After Sharon and Mr. Hill had read the letter, the three of them went on playing rummy without talking about it. After a few hands, Mr. Hill began asking them about their schoolwork, their friends, their apartment, even their parents. They found, to their surprise, that they could talk with him about their home and their parents without feeling miserable and homesick. They sounded just like old people talking about their lost youth.

Late in the evening, Tom asked about Aunt Eve. He wanted to know everything he could about her, where she was born, when she was born, what she had done, why she had come to the island, and, most of all, what kind of person she really was and why. Mr. Hill seemed glad to talk about her, but he felt he couldn't say too much.

"I don't want to tell you anything that she might want to tell you herself, but I'll tell you about the first time I met her, if you'd like. I used to be a doctor in Richmond, Virginia. I was a good doctor, considering the state of medicine in those days, and I was making a lot of money. There was a war on at the time, but I was too old for the army. I felt guilty, spending my time treating old people for rheumatism, getting money I didn't really need, when men were dying for want of simple care. Finally, when there were reports of bad fighting in western Virginia, I decided I'd try to do something. I had my wagon hitched, went to the hospital, borrowed a lot of instruments and bandages and medicines, asked a friend of mine to see after my practice, and drove west. I had a pair of beautiful gray horses then—they were stolen before I got back to Richmond—strong, intelligent, tough mares. Sisters.

"After six days of traveling, I came to a place where there had been fighting. Papers and letters were blowing around everywhere, a sure sign that men had been killed and their pockets searched for money before they were buried. When I got to the next town, there wasn't a bullet mark or a sign of fighting anywhere, but coming out of the open windows of the church I could hear coughing and moaning.

"Inside, the pews had been pushed and stacked against the walls and a lot of beds and cots moved in. It looked like a furniture junk yard, except that it was crowded with men. Leaning over one of the beds was your Aunt Eve. She was wearing a big white apron which had a lot of blood on it." Mr. Hill looked at Sharon as if he was afraid that the bloody apron might have shocked her. It hadn't.

"Your Aunt Eve wasn't a trained nurse, but she knew how to comfort the dying, and that was more than half her job. I introduced myself to her, and we began to make the rounds of the beds together. Other women came and went, but she stayed on, helping me put the wounded back together again. The next thing I knew, it was morning. I hadn't even noticed the night when it came."

Mr. Hill stopped, his mind and heart back in Virginia in the time of that terrible war. Clearly, he was telling them of the most important time in his life. "The thing I'll always remember," he said slowly, "was the sound of her voice—that soft, sure voice talking to those men and boys. We worked together for almost a week, without too much time for sleep, and when the dying had died, and the others were beginning to get well again, I said goodbye to her and took my wagon and a new pair of horses and went on. I didn't see her again for three years."

"How old was she then?" Tom asked.

"About the same age she is now."

"How long ago was that?" Sharon asked.

"You know the answer to that, Sharon." He got up. "Now I'm going to go home."

Sharon stood up too. "Would you like a cup of tea?" she asked, remembering that as the only woman in the house she had the duties of the hostess, and wanting him to stay until she felt sleepier, so she could go upstairs when he left and fall asleep right away. But he said no, thank you, he'd be glad to drink her tea another evening soon. Then he reminded them of their wet things, and Tom ran up to the bathroom, grabbed everything in the tub, including a damp washcloth, ran back down to the kitchen, pulled his soaking things off the back-porch railing, came back through the house, and handed them all to Mr. Hill, who rolled them into a ball under his arm. "I'd like to take you on a picnic tomorrow, if you'd like to come. I'd pick you up after breakfast."

"We'd like that," Tom said, and Sharon, in spite of herself, nodded.

"Good. We'll hike over to the south shore. It's very rocky there, and when the surf is high it's beautiful. Do you have enough blankets? There are extras in the upstairs hall closet, the one at the head of the stairs. Well, I'll say good night, then . . . No, I

won't either. There's one other thing I want to say
to you."

He stood with his back to the door. The bundle
of clothes under his arm was dripping on the hall
rug. "Your Aunt Eve is the best woman I've ever
known," he said. "It wasn't easy for her to decide to
kidnap you." He turned and opened the door. "Sleep
well. I'll see you after breakfast in the morning."

Tom stood holding the door. In his mind he could
see a church full of bleeding, bandaged soldiers.
Sharon stood wondering if Mr. Hill loved Aunt Eve,
and wondering, too, if he really understood her. He
disappeared into the shadow of the big tree in front
of his house, and Sharon turned away from the door.

"He doesn't walk like he's a hundred years old."

"That doesn't prove anything, the way a man
walks," Tom said. "He must be more than that. If
he was fifty during the Civil War, that would mean
that by now he must be . . ."

"I didn't say it proved anything," she said. "I was
just talking about the way he looks when he walks."
Tom shut the door. He was going to lock it, but it
had no lock. Then he went into the living room to
make sure the fire was quiet for the night and the
screen in place, and turned out the lights. The whole
house became dark, and they felt their way upstairs
by the light of the moon.

"I'm in no hurry," Sharon said when they got to
the top of the stairs. "You go in the bathroom first."

"O.K. I won't take long." He went into the bathroom and began to get ready for bed. While he was getting undressed, he remembered something Sharon had said to Mr. Hill while they were playing cards. Mr. Hill had asked them to say when they enjoyed being with their parents most. Without a moment's hesitation Sharon had said, "When we're talking," and then, right away, she had said, "I don't mean just talking talk, but really talking." Brushing his teeth, and watching himself in the mirror, Tom thought that her answer had been right, and that he probably wouldn't have thought of it. He finished and went into his room. Sharon was sitting on the end of his bed. She was still completely dressed. "You want to go in the bathroom? I'm through."

"No."

"Oh." Tom had a feeling that she wanted to say something, but didn't know how.

"Tom . . . I'm sorry I argued with you so much today."

"You didn't argue with me so much."

"Oh, yes, I did. I really didn't mean to."

". . . Why do you do things like that, Sharon?" he said. "Arguing about nothing. I just begin to think how much we're like each other, and then you start arguing with me about nothing."

"Maybe it's because I'm a girl," she said, but she didn't sound as if she believed it. Neither did Tom.

"That shouldn't make any difference," he said. "You know, I used to think sometimes that you were just like a brother."

"I want to be. I want to be a friend, anyway."

"Well, I still think you're pretty good," he said. "We'd better go to bed now. It's probably late." She got up and left. Five minutes later, when Tom was almost asleep, she came back.

"You know what I like about him?" she said, standing just inside the door. "He doesn't talk to you like you were a five-year-old."

"Neither does she," Tom answered, sleepy-voiced. Sharon turned and went back to her room without answering, and Tom, who hadn't opened his eyes, dropped off to sleep.

Sharon didn't. She lay with her eyes open for a long while, pulled back and forth by two strong impulses. One was the impulse to fight against Aunt Eve and try to get back home any way she could. The other impulse was to try to make the best of things. The same turn of mind which made her rush to the dentist when she had to go, now made her want to throw her whole self into the life Aunt Eve and Mr. Hill had forced on her.

She hated Aunt Eve, or nearly hated her, but she didn't hate Mr. Hill. She liked Mr. Hill. She liked him very much, even though he was part of the kidnapping. She wanted to please him, and impress him. When she saw Aunt Eve's face in her mind, she wanted to escape. When she saw Mr. Hill's, she wanted to stay.

When she fell asleep, she had a dream.

In her dream she was coming home from school and met Aunt Eve and Mr. Hill walking along Seventy-sixth Street. Aunt Eve was wearing a long dress with a lot of embroidery on it, and a wide-brimmed hat. Mr. Hill was wearing a very formal-looking dark suit with a red silk scarf. They had a German shepherd dog with them, on a leash, and the first thing they did was to give the dog to Sharon because he was a good hunter.

Then they invited her to a restaurant for strawberry ice cream, which they ate at a small table with a glass top and thin black legs with fancy feet.

Mr. Hill smiled at her, and then he and Aunt Eve got up and walked out.

Sharon and the dog followed them, and when she got out of the restaurant, which was also the drugstore on the corner near her apartment, Aunt Eve and Mr. Hill were gone. She wanted to go home, where she knew her father and mother were waiting for her, but instead she started looking for Aunt Eve and Mr. Hill. She saw them up the block and ran after them, but just when she had almost caught up with them, the dog refused to go on without some ice cream. So she went into a store and had some ice cream put on the floor for the dog. When he finished, he pulled her to the door and they went chasing after Aunt Eve and Mr. Hill again. Finally, she saw them holding hands and walking slowly along a street full of department stores, but the dog needed ice cream again, so she had to go into a department store and buy some from a shoe salesman who sold ice cream on the side, as a private business. She had to promise him she wouldn't tell anybody where she got it, before he'd give it to her.

By the time the dog had finished licking it off the floor, Aunt Eve and Mr. Hill were gone again. The dog started pulling her back the way they'd come, and then all of a sudden she knew that he wasn't really hunting Aunt Eve and Mr. Hill at all. But she was afraid to pull against him because he had gotten bigger and didn't look as friendly as he had at first, though he licked her hand every chance he got.

Then she met another man, a younger man, who looked like one of the teachers at school. He asked her what she was doing, and she told him she was trying to return this dog to its owners, who had lost it. He took her into his apartment and gave her some math problems to do in a small room. While she was doing them, she heard some talking in the living room, but she couldn't go there because she had the problems to do. Then the teacher came back and told her that he had advertised in the newspaper, and that Aunt Eve and Mr. Hill had just come and taken the dog away with them. "But it's my dog!" she shouted. "It's my dog! It's my dog!" A great tenderness welled up in her heart for her lost little dog who loved her, and she went straight out of the apartment and started walking fast up the street, looking for her dog and her aunt and her uncle.

She was in a part of the city that had been destroyed by bombs, and it was very quiet and peaceful. All the buildings had fallen down, but all the trees were still standing.

Then she knew that the dog was lying in front of the fire at Mr. Hill's house, waiting for her to come so that they could play. Just then she saw the water, which smelled wonderful, and she walked toward it. In the distance in front of her, she saw boats and a harbor. All she had to do was get a ticket and take a boat to the island and everything would be all right. She kept walking. The sea air smelled wonderful.

Then she woke up. It was dark. She went to the bathroom. On her way back, she stopped in the silent moonlit hall and listened. Far away she thought she could hear the whispery sound of the ocean against the shore, but she wasn't sure. It might have been the wind through the trees. She suddenly remembered the book of letters about her that was downstairs on Aunt Eve's desk, and for a moment she thought she might go get it and bring it upstairs and read it in bed, but she felt chilly and too sleepy. She went quietly into Tom's room to make sure he was still breathing, and then went back to bed and fell asleep right away.

When morning came, she had almost completely forgotten her dream. The only thing she could tell Tom was that she had had a crazy dream about a big dog who ate nothing but ice cream.

x 🌾🌾🌾

A Day, a Night

The picnic with Mr. Hill was miserable. They all
worked hard to enjoy themselves, and Mr. Hill
worked hardest of all, but the harder they worked,
the worse it got.

The day began with Sharon making a breakfast
of bread and butter and strawberry jam and milk.
Then Mr. Hill came over with a big picnic basket
and led them on a two-mile walk to the south end of

the island. The south end turned out to be a lot less dangerous and wild than they had hoped it would be. On the way they spent a lot of time thinking of things to say. Mr. Hill made some jokes, and they laughed at them, but they weren't funny.

They ate before noon, not because they were so hungry but because it gave them something to do. After lunch, Mr. Hill told them the names of all the rocks and grasses and bushes they could see. He knew the rules to a lot of games, so they tried to play them. He never seemed to tire of a game, so Tom had to be the one to say when it was over. Then Mr. Hill would say, "That was fun!" and they'd begin another game. It was awful.

They got back to the house late in the afternoon with sunburned necks. The wildflowers Sharon had picked were all wilted.

"That's the way he played rummy last night, too," Sharon said sadly as she and Tom sat in the living room.

"How's that?" Tom asked. He didn't sound very interested.

"He played as if he was just following the rules and not really playing at all. . . . He played just like Bobby Seller."

"Who's he?" Tom said as he stretched out on the rug in front of the cold fireplace.

"You know him, he's in my class. He always plays games as if they were arithmetic problems, with his tongue stuck out between his teeth."

"One part was all right," Tom said after a while. "When he showed us the electric generator. I'll bet it takes a barge full of coal every two months just to keep the boiler going."

Sharon had always somehow had the idea that electric generators ran on electricity, and though she knew that wasn't true, she wasn't especially interested in finding out what they *did* run on. She wouldn't have walked across the room to see the most beautiful steam-driven electric generator in the world.

"I felt sorry for him," she said, trying to get back on the subject of their terrible picnic. "He's such a nice man."

"He sure doesn't know how to play," Tom said, and then they both were quiet for a while. Sharon got up from the couch and went over to the desk and stared at the loose-leaf book with SHARON printed on the front of it. She wanted to read the letters "J.H." had written about her, and yet at the same time she didn't want to read them, because she wasn't sure what she'd find in them. She was about to ask Tom to let her look at his book, but then he'd want to look at hers, and she didn't want him to. She turned away and looked at the bookshelves in the wall. On the bottom shelf, lying flat, were eight volumes of *The Boston Recorder, A Weekly Newspaper,* bound like oversized books in dark brown leather. Each volume had a date on it. The bottom one was dated 1842 and the top one 1849. She pulled the one marked

1845 out of the middle. It was so heavy it almost dropped on the floor.

"I think I'll go upstairs and read," she said.

"O.K." Tom looked over at her. "What's that big book?"

"Just a lot of old newspapers. I'm just looking at it. Tell me if you think about going out."

"O.K. You're not hungry, are you?" he said.

"Not especially. Are you?"

"Not especially," he said, though he would have been glad at the chance to eat, anyway.

It would have been something to do.

Sharon went out of the room and Tom lay on the floor for a while. Then he got up and went over to the desk. He wanted to read at least one of the letters about Sharon so much it made him feel ashamed of himself, which made him want to all the more. He opened her book in a casual kind of way, as if he weren't really interested in it but only idling through it on his way somewhere else. Then he closed it easily, picked it up, walked over to the couch, and sat down.

He put the book down next to him and listened. He couldn't hear anything. Then he picked the book up and riffled through its pages. When he came to the last letter, he stopped.

Dear Eve,

I'm well, and busy, dividing my time be-tween watching the children, reading at the Medical Center library, and seeing after the taxes on the Fund. There are two open lectures at the Medical Center next Monday and Tuesday, and I'll be staying for them. That will bring me home again on March 1, unless something else comes up.

Eve, if we're really convinced that the island needs children and would be good for them, this summer will be the time to take Tom and Sharon. I wrote you about Tom a few days ago. Now let me sum up what I think about Sharon, pro and con:

1. She is physically strong.
2. She is intelligent.
3. She is responsible.
4. She is imaginative and independent, can entertain herself for long periods alone.
5. She is vain, easily persuaded by attractive clothes that she is beautiful, which by common standards she is not.
6. She becomes unreasonable when she is upset or thwarted.
7. Her kindness and interest in others have a lot of plain animal curiosity in them.
8. She is selfish (that is to say, she is human), and, finally, she is charming.

That's all from me for now.

As ever, J.H.

Tom leaned back against the couch and closed his eyes and thought, or at least tried to think. Why, he wondered, did the island need children? And what "good" could the island do them? He wanted to talk to Sharon about it, but first he would have to tell her he had read part of her book. He remembered how mad he had been the night before, when he had thought she was reading in his. Well, he'd just have to tell her and say he was sorry and let her be mad.

"Sharon?" he yelled.

"Don't go without me, I'll come right down."

"I'm not going anywhere."

"What?"

"I'm not going anywhere. I just wanted to tell you I read one of the letters in your book."

"We'll eat in a little while, O.K.?" Sharon called down, and Tom realized that she hadn't understood him. The house became absolutely still. He got up, put her book back on the desk, went to the window, and stared out.

Upstairs, sprawled on her bed, Sharon was lost in *The Boston Recorder* of 1845. The paper was yellow and very brittle—the first page she turned broke off along its bound edge—but in spite of being afraid that the whole thing would fall apart in her hands, she kept turning the pages and reading, fascinated. *The Boston Recorder*, she soon found out, had been an anti-slavery newspaper. On one page there was an article about some people who had been arrested for helping slaves escape. One person on the list caught her attention.

MISS DELIA A. WEBSTER. If the Louisville Courier and Tribune are correct, she has been tried an 1 found guilty by a Kentucky jury. If so, the penitentiary will have to make room for the fair sufferer.

That was all the article said about her, but it was enough to excite Sharon's imagination. How had Delia Webster been helping slaves escape? How had she been caught? Was she young or old? (That question was easy to answer. She was young, and probably beautiful.) Was she working alone? How long was she going to have to stay in prison?

The words "fair sufferer" sounded so old-fashioned to Sharon, but they moved her feelings just the same. She envied Delia, and felt poorer for never having known her. She yearned to know more about her, and enjoyed the bittersweet knowledge that she never would.

She mourned for Delia, long in her grave.

From the editorial page of the issue for January 2, 1845, she learned that there had been heavy rains in Italy in December. The Tiber had overflowed its banks, flooding the lower sections of the city of Rome. She read that a group of the representatives of the Danish states had petitioned the King of Denmark to end slavery in the Danish colonies. Sharon wondered what the Danish colonies were. Iceland and Greenland? Were there slaves in Iceland and Greenland? On the same page she read that the Czar of Russia had issued an order prohibiting all Polish males under the age of thirty from marrying. She

read about the illness of Madame Rothschild, 99
years old, whose eldest son had promised the poor a
sum of 40,000 florins "if his mother accomplished her
100th year." Sharon wondered if the old lady had
made it, and if she had, whether her son had kept his
promise, and how.

She read on and on, completely absorbed in the
world of 1845. She read notices of marriages, and
births, and deaths, as if the people marrying, and
having babies, and dying were members of her own
family. She read notices of a hundred public meet-
ings, and wanted to attend them all. She read an
advertisement for "a concert performance on the
piano by Madame Pauline Glayas," and could hear
the music. For the first time in her life, the past became alive to her. It felt closer than anything.

As the late afternoon sun rained gold into her
bedroom, her heart beat in another century, the century of Delia A. Webster.

After a long while, she got hungry. She hated to
turn away from 1845, but as the only woman in the
house, she knew it was her duty to fix something
to eat, so she went downstairs. She went into the
kitchen, with Tom right behind her, and put out
bread and butter and jam and milk. For dessert they
ate a quart jar of home-canned peaches.

And then it was dark.

They went into the living room and Tom started
the fire. Their necks burned from the day in the sun,
but still they felt chilly, and the fire didn't seem to

help. Both of them yawned a few times, but neither of them wanted to go to bed. Sharon decided to go upstairs and take a long hot bath.

"I think I'll go upstairs and sit in the tub."

"O.K. I'm going to go out for a while."

"You mean alone? Where?"

"I don't know, just around. I won't be long."

"I don't think you should."

"Why not?"

"I don't know, I just don't think you should. You don't know what you might find out there."

"Like what?"

"I don't know what." Sharon stopped thinking about having a bath, and stopped feeling chilly. Tom got up from in front of the fireplace and started toward the stairs.

"I guess I ought to wear a sweater," he said, trying to sound very sensible.

"You going alone?" Sharon asked again.

"You want to come with me?"

"Well, I don't want you to go alone. I don't know what I'd do here all by myself, anyway."

"Have a bath."

"I don't want a bath, I'm clean enough as it is . . . I'll get your sweater, too," she said. She was halfway up the stairs.

A minute later, they were standing at the front door.

"Let's go out the back door," he said.

"Why?"

He shrugged, and the two of them went through the dining room, into the kitchen, and out the back door, closing it quietly behind them. Then they walked around to the front of the house and started walking down the middle of Main Street toward the village. That way anyone watching them—and they were sure someone was watching all the time—would know that they weren't trying to sneak around.

Just to have something to say, Sharon said, "I haven't seen any cats."

"I haven't seen any dogs, either," Tom said. "Maybe it's part of their religion not to have them."

"You really think so?"

"Probably the only things they have are snakes."

"Have you seen any snakes?" Sharon asked.

"None big enough to worry about," he said, grinning in spite of himself.

Soon they came to the *Islander* office. They stopped and looked at the front page in the window. They could easily read the headlines by the moonlight, NEWCOMERS ARRIVE on the right and THE WISE HOST on the left. Remembering that they were Greeks among Trojans made them feel closer to one another, and somehow stronger.

"I read one of the letters in your book this afternoon, the last one," Tom confessed as they stood looking at the paper.

"That's all right." she said.

"I just wanted you to know. You can look at mine anytime you want to."

"Really, I don't mind your reading it," she said. She didn't want to be angry with Tom. Not now, anyway.

"Look, the door's open."

It was open, with a wedge under it to hold it open. They went in slowly, Tom first. The office was full of shadows, which made it seem higher and bigger than it really was. The walls had recently been painted a glossy light brown, and the place still smelled of paint, or maybe it was only the ink that smelled.

In the middle of the room stood a printing press the size of a big automobile, but higher. A heavy wooden desk sat against the righthand wall. There were some papers on it covered with tiny handwriting. Next to the desk was a big grandfather's clock, with no hands. It was ticking.

In the back of the office a dim lightbulb with a green metal shade on it hung from the ceiling. Under it was a long table with another, smaller printing press on it. Under the table were some big open cardboard boxes. The boxes were full of money.

Neither Tom nor Sharon knew what to say. Nothing came to mind that seemed quite right. For a moment Tom was going to say, "Look at these boxes full of money," but he didn't. They stood together silently for what seemed like a long time, while inside their heads greed and surprise and awe and fear and curiosity scrambled through some games of musical chairs.

They moved closer.

The money was gathered into small packages held together by narrow strips of brown paper. The packages were arranged neatly in the boxes, face down, light green side up. The money green was the only attractive color in the room. One box had twenties, another tens, another fives, and two boxes had ones.

In a little while Tom and Sharon's awe and greed and surprise and fear faded away and they were left with their curiosity. Was this, they asked themselves, the place where Aunt Eve came to pick up their Christmas presents? Was Mr. Eliot wanted by the FBI? Was the money left there just to test them, and if so, were they being watched through a peephole in the ceiling? They began to want to leave right away, before someone jumped out from somewhere behind them. Still, they didn't move, either toward the money or away from it.

But it wasn't their fear of being caught, or even their honesty, which kept them from touching the money in the five cardboard boxes. It was indifference. Either one of them would have scrubbed a whole house to get ten dollars, but a thick package of twenties, or even of ones, was more money than either of them wanted to touch. Like cats, who instinctively avoid eating so much food that they will have to vomit, Tom and Sharon instinctively disdained the fat packages of money. They turned and walked slowly out of the office.

They both wanted to go back to the house, but not right away. First they wanted to let whoever might be watching them know that they weren't excited or frightened, so they walked easily across the street to "The Jewel Movie Palace" and looked at the poster out in front. The theater was showing a movie called *Goodbye Broadway, Hello Arizona!* The poster showed a round-faced tap dancer in a spangled bathing suit dancing while pressing her cheek against the cheek of a smiling cowboy whose hat was on crooked. Tom and Sharon looked at it awhile in the pale moonlight, and then walked slowly back to Aunt Eve's house.

When they got there, they found a basket of washed and ironed clothes in front of the door. A note was pinned on top, written in big letters with a thick pen.

Sorry I missed you. Dinner tomorrow?
                                          Mr. Hill

Sharon opened the door and Tom carried the basket inside and started up the stairs.

"You want to go?" he asked.

"I guess so," Sharon said in an offhand way, trying not to show how much she wanted to go, or how strongly she felt the need for Mr. Hill's protection.

She wished he was sleeping in the house with them.

As he settled himself for sleep, Tom realized with a rush of shame that he hadn't thought about his parents all day. Here he was going on picnics and wandering around at night playing detective and not thinking of his poor mother and father at all. And maybe he hadn't thought of them yesterday either. Had he thought of them the day before that? Probably. After all, that was . . . What day was that, anyway? Saturday? Yes, Saturday. He must have thought of them at least once on Saturday. And come to think of it, he and Sharon had talked about them for quite a while on Sunday morning, too, as they sat on the dock. So, that wasn't so bad, was it? No, not at all.

Still, he didn't miss them much, or feel sorry for them, most of the time.

By now he was wide awake. It came to him that since he was a prisoner he should be planning to escape. He'd secretly build a raft. Then, late one silent, moonless night, he and Sharon would sneak out to where they had hidden it, push it off into the calm sea, hoist sail, and sail off at a good steady speed for the mainland. He could see them two days later, sunburned but healthy, sailing into some medium-sized harbor while people stared at them from motorboats and docks, and wondered who they were, and admired their daring and coolness.

He got out of bed, went over to the small desk next to his closet, found a piece of paper and pencil, and began to design his raft. It should be made, he de-

cided, of at least ten fairly big logs tied together—
he'd find the rope somewhere, or make it out of vines.
It should have a little cabin in the middle, with a
roof of birchbark, and a hole in the front for a mast,
which could be made from a straight pine tree with
the branches knocked off. They could make the sail
out of four bedsheets, which Sharon could sew together for thickness and strength on the night they
left. Of course it would take time to build, but they'd
be able to find a place to hide it while they were
working on it.

He looked at his pencil sketch. It looked pretty
good, except for the cabin, which looked a little
flimsy. They'd have to work on the cabin a lot and
strengthen it. The whole job might take them all
summer. He wrote on the bottom of the picture:
SAILING DATE, SEPTEMBER 15, AT NIGHT. Then he hid
the picture under the linoleum on the floor of the
closet.

Back in bed, without the picture to look at, he
began to have doubts. His doubts didn't come from
fear—he was hardly at all afraid of taking the raft
to sea—but he just wasn't sure he really wanted to
go. So again sadness and anger at himself washed
over him, and shame. He was sure that Sharon
wanted terribly to get away as soon as possible, that
she missed their parents and wanted to go home more
than anything else in the world. He felt awful that
he should be the one who didn't care, at least most
of the time, about the way his parents felt. He de-

cided to begin the raft right away. Working hard on it would be his way of saying "I'm sorry" to his parents for being so selfish. He would escape at the end of the summer, for Sharon's sake and for the sake of his parents. He got up again, went to the desk, lighted the light, took the sketch out from under the closet linoleum, and drew in a rudder. Then he put it back, turned off the light, and fell asleep.

Sharon was still wide awake. The impulse to fight against her fate, and the impulse to throw herself into it, were at war again, as they had been the night before. She turned over for the fifteenth time, sure that Tom's mind was much less confused than hers, that he knew exactly what he wanted to do, and that made her feel ashamed.

Finally, though, she too fell asleep.

xi

They Build a City

Some mornings Tom liked to let himself drift between sleeping and waking, like a bird floating with its eyes shut into a warm and gentle wind. That's what he did for a while after the sun came up the next morning—he drifted between sleep and the day, waiting for his mother to come to his bed, put her hand on his shoulder, and say, "Time to get up, Tom."

She had an old green corduroy robe which she wore every morning, and as he began coming awake he could almost smell it. But as he woke up more, the robe faded from the room, carrying his mother away with it, and finally he was left awake with a terrible longing for her and home. Then he heard Sharon moving around downstairs.

"What have you been doing?" he called out.

"Reading the book of letters about you and making breakfast. I'm sure Mr. Hill wrote them. Who else could J.H. be?"

"Are you reading now?"

"It wasn't very interesting, so I put it back."

"Oh." He stretched. The floor felt cold on his feet. As he got dressed, he wondered if there was any letter in particular she thought was uninteresting, or if she thought all of them were. It was hard for him to believe that all of them could be uninteresting. After all, he was a fairly interesting sort of person. In fact, very interesting.

"Your toast is getting cold," Sharon called up from the kitchen. He tied his sneakers and went down. She had set the dining-room table with good china and silverware. There was orange juice, butter on a crystal butter dish, a silver tray with four kinds of jam and jelly, and another silver tray with toast. "I've had the toast in the oven keeping warm," she said. "And I'm frying eggs." He could hear them sizzling. "Sit down, almost everything's ready."

"Why did you do all this?"

"I don't know . . . I didn't feel very good when

I woke up, so I thought that maybe if I got up and did something, it would be better." A few moments later she came out with two plates. On each plate there were two fried eggs, looking as good as any fried eggs he had ever seen.

"Why didn't you feel good?"

She shrugged. "I was just thinking about home. Not that it's any use." She sat down quickly and looked down at her plate. They ate without talking. When they were through, Tom said, "Let's go to the beach."

Both of them remembered that they had a dinner date with Mr. Hill, but neither of them spoke of it.

They cleared off the table, put the dishes in the sink, and started out the front door. Just as he was shutting it, Tom said, "Just a second," opened it again, and ran back inside. He went to the kitchen and grabbed a quart jar of plums, a brown paper bag, a box of matches, and two teaspoons, from various drawers and cupboards. By the time he got out the door, he had put everything in the bag. He waved it in front of her face and said, "Lunch!"

"What is it?"

"Food fit for a king."

"What kind of food is that?"

"Royal food . . . Come on." He led the way around to the back of the house, through the back yard, and up the grassy hill beyond which lay the sea. When they reached the top of the hill, they began running. The smell of the blue sea air made them almost feel as if they could fly.

When they got to the beach, they threw themselves down and watched the sea. The beach was very flat and wide, made of fine, almost white sand with a lot of small, mostly smooth stones in it. The tide was coming in. After a while, leaving the bag and their sneakers and socks under a twisted pine tree, they went down to the water and slowly walked along the hard wet sand across which low waves spilled and slid, spilled and slid, spilled and slid.

By the time they turned back, the sky was full of heavy clouds. Their pockets and hands were full of beautiful shells and stones, and their heads under the gray glare of noon were almost dizzy from watching the continual coming and going of the water at their feet. When they got back to their pine tree, they lay down under it and rested for a while. Then Tom sat up and started idly digging at the sand with a shell. Sharon rolled onto her side and looked easily around.

Lying there, her head against her arm, she looked as if she had been born on that beach, as if her amber eyes knew every stone on it and every wave that hit it. And for a few minutes that's how she felt, as if she were an eternal part of the sand and the stones and the sea.

Tom suddenly got up and ran down to the water to rescue a long, blackened board which was washing back and forth. He dragged it a good distance away from the water, dropped it on the dry sand, and yelled to Sharon.

"Let's build a city."

She got up right away and ran to him, brushing off her dungarees as she went. They set to work. First they built a front wall by putting the board in the sand, edge down, and piling sand on both sides of it. Behind the wall they ran a wide road. Then Sharon built a big square building out of wet sand, while he built side walls. Then they made two narrower roads running from the wall to their big building, which now had a stick flagpole and was the City Hall. They built two more buildings near the wall and put up watchtowers. Then Sharon got some beach grasses and thatched the roofs of the smaller buildings and Tom set to work paving the roads with stones.

When the city was done, Tom went to the tree and got the jar of plums and the spoons. After banging the metal lid with a stone for a long time, he finally got it unscrewed.

"Let's eat."

They stood together looking over their city and taking turns spooning plums out of the jar. The plums were warm, and the red-purple juice dribbled down onto their white sweat shirts, so that by the time the jar was empty it looked as if they had been drinking wine from a fountain.

They sat down and rested. They were relaxing by their city, not particularly looking at anything, when the edge of a wave touched the front wall and disappeared into the sand. "The tide's coming in," Tom said quickly, and they set to work to protect their city.

First they repaired the slight damage to the front wall, and built it higher. The front edge of another wave slid into the wall and even came along the sides for a foot or so, but the city inside stayed dry. While Tom ran the side walls farther back, Sharon put stones around City Hall. Another wave came, and this time some water splashed over the front wall and uncovered part of the board. While he was covering it up again, another wave took away more sand.

By now they knew that the city was going to be washed away, but they worked on it anyway, busy with a growing excitement and joy. It was Tom and Sharon against the incoming tide, and they were determined to hold it off by work and cleverness and will power for at least one more wave. A big one came, and the road behind the wall suddenly became a canal. Soon water was turning the corner of the side walls and coming in the back. Sharon began to build a rear wall while Tom got some big stones to help keep the front wall from collapsing. He was kneeling in front of the wall with a heavy stone in each hand when a wave smashed into it, washed through most of the city, and took off the front half of City Hall. All the other buildings were just wet lumps of sand. Sharon started to fix City Hall while Tom tried to set the front board more firmly into the sand by banging it with his biggest stone.

And then it was all over. The sea was around them, and the whole city was awash. The board in the front wall was loose again, and the stones in the streets were either loose or buried in the sand. But the sea had been kept back for a short time, and Tom and Sharon felt like conquerors. By the time the last bit of wall was washed flat by the sea, they had already left the city behind and were running down the beach playing tag.

Late in the afternoon, a light but steady wind came up, and Tom built a fire near the pine tree. It was a big fire made out of driftwood, and it burned hot in the wind. Their dungarees and sweat shirts dried out in its heat, and they put their sneakers and socks back on. They sat and stared at the fire, and every once in a while Tom added a piece of wood or rearranged what was burning with a long stick. Neither of them wanted to leave, not because they didn't want to go to Mr. Hill's for dinner—in fact, they were both very hungry—but because they didn't want to leave the day behind them. But after a while, by silent agreement, Tom stopped feeding the fire and they watched it fall to coals in the wind.

"Let's go home. I'm hungry."

"O.K."

They covered the coals with sand and walked away as the tide began to go down again.

On their way home they realized how late it was. The sun had set and part of the sky was already dark. They decided it would be better to go to Mr. Hill's right away instead of changing their clothes first. He was delighted to see them, and didn't seem to mind at all how sloppy they looked. They ate and ate and ate, and excused themselves as soon as they could after helping him wash the dishes. When they got in the house, they went right upstairs. Sharon went into her room and turned on the light, and Tom came in after her. Pinned on her pillow was a pink envelope. She unpinned it and opened it up. The letter inside had been typed on a not very good typewriter. It said:

Dear Sharon,

When we were young, there were certain rules of behavior we were expected to follow:

1. Children were expected to dress properly on Sunday and every other day.
2. Children were expected to keep out of places where they had not been invited by adults.
3. Children were expected to be home after dark.
4. Children were forbidden to start fires or to play with matches.

These are only a few of the simple, sensible rules every child ought to follow *without exception.* Before you arrived, we were led to believe that you had been well brought up and properly disciplined to know your place. We hope that we have not been deceived, and that your *undisciplined* and *impolite* behavior in the past few days is only temporary, due to the absence of your Guardian.

However, do not mistake our goodhearted understanding for foolishness. We *cannot allow unchildlike behavior* here on our Island. It is folly not to punish a child who needs it for the good of its character.

We hope that you sleep well tonight and have the happy dreams all children ought to have, and that you will awaken tomorrow with a smile on your face and resolutions in your heart to behave in the future as a good child should.

Very sincerely yours,
Some Friends

"Look, they even remade my bed," Sharon said, "and I made it perfectly before I made breakfast this morning."

"I wonder if I've got a note too," Tom said, and left the room. The word "outrageous" came into Sharon's mind again. Then she realized that Tom was gone, and she didn't want to be alone, so she went after him. "They made my bed too," he said as she came in. "It makes me glad I didn't." In his hand was a blue sheet of paper. "I got the same note you did."

Sharon was still thinking about her bed. "I worked hard making it, too," she said. "As if I couldn't make my own bed. We didn't ask to come here . . . We should go and set a real fire somewhere." She began to cry. "They didn't need to make my bed as if I was a baby."

"Don't pay any attention to it, Sharon. They don't know what they're talking about." She sat down on the end of his bed with her head down. He sat next to her and put his hand on her shoulder. It didn't seem to help. He got up. "I wonder how many of them helped write it. It can't be very many."

"How do you know?" she said in the angry tone of voice she always got when she was crying. "It might be that everybody hates us."

"You think we should show it to Aunt Eve?" he asked, just to have something to say.

"I don't know . . . We didn't ask to come here."

"Don't worry, Sharon, it'll be all right."

"We could have fun if they'd leave us alone."

"I know what I'll do, Sharon. I'll go downtown and put a big sign up in the newspaper office window, WE'LL DO WHATEVER WE LIKE, and sign it."

She looked over at him with fear in her eyes. "You wouldn't really do it, would you? I don't think you ought to go out at all."

"I won't," he said. "I'll stay right here."

"I wish Mr. Hill was here so we weren't alone," Sharon said. "Even Aunt Eve would be better than nobody. At least she doesn't *hate* us." She got up and went into the bathroom and shut the door. A few minutes later, she came out in her pajamas with her face washed. "They hung my pajamas in the bath-room, on two hangers," she said, and started to laugh.

"Probably so you wouldn't get mixed up and put the wrong part on the wrong end," he said. He was happy to see her laugh, and laughed with her.

"They've got yours on two hangers too," she said.

"You know what I should do?" he said. "I should go and get some charcoal from the fire and write on all the houses, THE GREEKS WERE HERE."

Sharon stopped laughing.

"I'm not going to do it," Tom said, seeing the worry come back into her face, "but I ought to."

"They'd think of some way of getting back at us," she said. "Some real mean way." She was quiet for a few minutes. "I'm sure glad you're here," she said. "If you weren't here, I don't know what I'd do."

"I'm glad I'm here, too," he said, and right away he felt silly for saying it. "I think I'll get ready for bed." He started out of the room.

"I wonder if Aunt Eve will tell Mom and Dad the truth," Sharon said when he was almost to the door.

"I don't know."

"I bet she will, but she'll make it so they won't be able to do anything about it."

Tom went into the bathroom and got ready for bed. When he came out, Sharon was out of his room, in her own, and asleep. He went quietly downstairs and got his book of letters off the desk in the dark-ened living room. He was very tired, but before he went to sleep he wanted to read just one or two of the letters Mr. Hill had written about him. He brought the book upstairs, got into bed, and started to read.

The letters were dull, just as Sharon had said they were, and in a few minutes he put the book on the floor, turned off the light, and lay back with his hands under his head. His mind drifted back to their day on the beach, and to the city they had built and saved, for a time, from the incoming tide. It had been a good city. Then he remembered the note from "Some Friends," and his jaw tightened. Mean. Stupid. Cruel. Stupid. Hanging up pajamas on different hangers. Stupid. He shook his head, turned over, and tried to forget how stupid grownups can be.

xii

Aunt Eve Comes Home

The next morning, right after breakfast, Tom and
Sharon went down to meet Aunt Eve. They wanted
to kiss her and be kissed by her in front of as many
people as possible, so that everybody would know
that she was on their side.

They were disappointed when they got to the dock
because no one was there, not even Mr. Hill. They
decided that maybe he knew exactly when she was
coming and would arrive just before she got there,

so they watched in two directions, out to sea for Aunt Eve and back up Harbor Road for Mr. Hill.

Aunt Eve came, but Mr. Hill didn't.

The first sight they had of the barge was just before noon. Soon they could see Aunt Eve clearly, standing behind the rail that ran around the pilot-house. She waved, and they waved back.

"What did you say she said when she called up Friday?" Sharon asked when they were through waving and Aunt Eve had gone back into the pilothouse.

"She just said we were changing plans, and we should come down right away and not bring anything and she'd be waiting for us outside in her car."

"Oh."

Sharon was quiet for a while, looking out to sea, and then she said, "I don't think we should tell her about the notes we got last night."

"Why not?" Tom asked.

"I just don't think we should," Sharon said. "At least not right away. We can always tell her later."

"I don't like not telling her," Tom said, but from his tone of voice when he said it—he had that tone people get in their voices when they're agreeing to do something they don't really want to do—Sharon understood that he wouldn't say anything, at least not right away.

Now the barge was much closer, but not yet close enough to call to. Tom's back started to itch. Sharon felt terribly alone. She longed to go home.

"Good morning, Mistress Sharon, Master Thomas.

It looks to be a lovely day, don't you think?" They turned around. Mr. Eliot, who had come quietly up the dock behind them, tipped his hard straw hat toward Sharon. "I see you've come to meet your aunt. How nice. That's the kind of thing children are best at. Oh, you look just like a picture in a magazine. Yes, if I were an artist I'd paint you just the way you are now, standing on this dock with your sweet little faces turned toward the sea. May I say in the Sunday edition that you came to the pier on Wednesday morning, happily anticipating a joyful reunion with your dear aunt?"

They both wanted to look him straight in the eye and say no, loudly, but they said nothing.

They turned away and looked toward the barge again. It was quite close now, almost next to them. Its motor grew quiet for a few moments, and then there was a big rumble, and the water churned. The barge hung back a moment and then pressed into the dock, making a great creaking noise. The motor stopped. Homer Patience worked the gangplank into place and began tying the barge up. A moment later Aunt Eve walked onto the dock. She looked tired and worn, but she smiled at them, and they could see that she was glad to be back with them. They went to her, but for some reason they didn't kiss her or put their arms around her.

The three, not touching, started walking slowly back along the dock toward home. No one said a word.

In a few steps they came up to Mr. Eliot, who was smiling a smile that even he seemed to realize was too big. He had the newspaper in his hand.

"I've brought you a copy of the Sunday edition," he said, taking half an inch off his smile but keeping the other three inches firmly in place.

"Thank you very much, Mr. Eliot," she said, took the paper, and started to walk on.

"I wonder if a few of us might have a talk with you this evening, at my house," Mr. Eliot said quietly.

"I'd be delighted to see you, Mr. Eliot," she answered. "My house is always open."

"We had thought that perhaps my house would be more suitable," Mr. Eliot said.

"I've been away from my niece and nephew too long already," Aunt Eve said. "I'm afraid I couldn't possibly leave them this evening."

"It's very important," Mr. Eliot said.

"Then by all means do come and visit me, and bring as many friends as you like." She paused and looked at him hard. "We'll serve tea."

"Perhaps, then, after the dear children are asleep," Mr. Eliot said, "we will come."

"At your convenience, Mr. Eliot, at your convenience," Aunt Eve said, and started moving again. When they were a little distance from him, she said, "I'm glad to see you. I think you're getting suntanned already . . . I'll tell you about my trip this afternoon. Right now I'm just a little too tired to start. I'll tell you everything after I take a nap."

Tom turned around to see if Mr. Eliot was behind them. The street was empty, which made the houses seem alive.

When they got home, Aunt Eve said to Sharon, "I wonder if you'd make me a cup of tea, Sharon, and bring it to my room?" Sharon was glad to have something to do. She worked as quickly as she could, boiling water and filling a big teapot and putting it, with a cup and saucer, sugar, and four wedges of lemon, on a wooden tray. Tom offered to carry it up for her, but Sharon wanted to do it herself. He went up the stairs with her, and a few moments later they were sitting on the end of Aunt Eve's bed, watching her sip tea with lemon but no sugar.

After a while she began to talk, but not about her visit with their mother and father. She talked about paintings. "I went to the Metropolitan Museum while I was in New York," she said. She handed Sharon a postcard with a reproduction of an old painting on it. It showed a fourteen- or fifteen-year-old girl standing next to her bedroom window. She was wearing a blue dress with a fine lace collar. Next to her was a dark wood bureau with a marble top. A white pitcher and bowl stood on it. The girl wasn't looking at anything, or doing anything.

She was simply absorbed in being herself.

"Isn't she lovely?" Aunt Eve said. She wasn't asking a question, she was paying a tribute. "I think she's a miracle."

"It's a beautiful picture," Sharon said, passing it across the foot of the bed to Tom. He looked at it, thought it was very nice, and handed it back to Aunt Eve. "Maybe we should let you go to sleep now," he said. "You're right," Aunt Eve said. "I should go to sleep now." They got off her bed. "I'll sleep until late afternoon. Mr. Patience will be bringing my suitcase by in a little while. Have him put it in the front hall downstairs, and ask him please to hold the ferry because I'm sending him a passenger this evening."

Tom took the tray gently off her lap. "And, if you don't mind, I'd prefer you didn't go out this afternoon." They went through the door, and Sharon, whose hands were free, quietly closed it. They stood there until Tom said, "Want to play some rummy?" and then they started down the stairs.

Late Wednesday afternoon, Aunt Eve sat down over tea with Tom and Sharon and Mr. Hill. The children were tense, and Sharon's longing to get away hadn't left her. Aunt Eve seemed tense too.

She asked them what had happened while she was away. They told her about going to hear Mr. Simpson, about the rainstorm that soaked them on Sunday afternoon, about Sunday evening's card game with Mr. Hill, about Monday's picnic with him, and about their day on the beach by themselves. All this took them less than three minutes, and when they were through, the things that they hadn't told her about crowded into their minds—Mr. Eliot's editorial, Mr. Hill's story of his first meeting with her, the money in the cardboard boxes at the *Islander* office, the threatening notes on their beds, and the feeling that everyone on the island was an enemy. Except for mentioning their day on the beach, they didn't tell her about anything that mattered to them at all, and they knew that she knew that they were keeping a lot back.

Then she began to tell them about her time in New York.

"I phoned your apartment from LaGuardia airport right after I arrived Sunday evening, and talked to your father. His voice was firm, and he spoke sensibly. He told me that he had called the police early Friday evening—there was a policeman beside him then, he said—but that they had no clues as to where you were. They assumed that you had been kidnapped.

"I told him that I didn't want to keep him on the phone, and asked if he or your mother could meet me at the Plaza. He said yes, right away, probably because he hoped I could furnish some ransom money if it were needed. I said I hoped it wouldn't be necessary for a policeman to come too, and he said no, whoever came would come alone."

"No need to bring a policeman just for a friendly visit with good old Aunt Eve," Sharon said to herself.

"Your mother was at the hotel when I got there. She was neatly dressed, and she even smiled for a moment when we shook hands, but she looked like a person with a high fever: wide-eyed and restless and confused. I told her when we got to my room that I knew where you both were, and that you were well and safe."

Sharon tried to get in her mind a picture of how her mother must have looked at that moment. She briefly caught sight of her in her imagination, sitting, leaning forward as if to hear better, with her lips slightly apart. But the picture faded right away.

"I gave her the clothes you were wearing on Friday, and the photograph Mr. Rice took of you on Saturday, which was very good. She looked at the photograph closely, and then she told me she wanted to phone your father and have him come to the hotel. I told her that if she did I would have to leave immediately. Then I told her that you would be free to return to New York, if you wished, on September 15, but that you probably would choose to remain here."

Tom and Sharon each took a bite of oatmeal cookie, chewed, and swallowed. Sharon sipped some tea, which was only warm. Tom said, "You mean

that after September 15 we can go or stay, which-
ever we want?"

"Yes. Kidnapping you was cruel enough. Keeping
you permanently, against your will, would be still
more cruel. It would also be pointless."

"School begins on the ninth, doesn't it?" Sharon
asked.

"I think so," Tom said. "I don't know."

"Yes, it does," Aunt Eve said.

"Why the fifteenth?" Tom said. "Is something happening on the fifteenth?"

"No," Aunt Eve said. "I said the fifteenth because
by that time you'll be used to being away from home.
If you miss your parents at all by then, it will only
be for a few moments at a time once in a while.
You'll be completely used to the island, to this house,
to the routine of our day, and to me. And you'll have
learned to appreciate the special chance you have
here, which you would not and could not have anywhere in the world."

"What chance?" Tom asked.

"The chance to stay exactly as you are right now
—never to have to grow old and die."

In the silence Sharon tried to look as calm as the
young woman in the picture Aunt Eve had shown
her. She thought again of her mother sitting in the
hotel room with Aunt Eve, and wondered why she
hadn't gotten up out of her chair, run to the phone,
and called the police. Or why she hadn't just gotten

up, grabbed Aunt Eve's arm, and shouted for help? Aunt Eve looked at her.

"Your mother didn't call the police, Sharon, because I told her that I was taking a life-preserving drug, that I had only two tablets with me, that if I was arrested I would tell nothing, and that without the drug I would probably die."

"Did she believe you?" Tom asked.

"Of course she did. I was telling the truth. I tried to assure her as firmly as possible that you were well, and not being harmed. She kept asking me in different ways to let you go, and I kept telling her you would be free at noon on September 15. She asked if she could talk to you on the phone, and I said no. She asked for more photographs, and I told her I didn't have any. She asked me to describe where you were staying, and I said no. She asked me to bring you a letter from her, and I said no."

"Why?" Tom asked.

"Because she has nothing important to say to you that she hasn't already said."

"How do you know?" Tom asked, not so much angry as curious.

"She's had you both now for a long time. If she hasn't told you the important things yet, she hasn't any important things to tell."

"Then what happened?" Sharon asked.

"I told her I had to go, and she asked me to stay another minute. I could see she was wondering if she shouldn't hold me and try to get the police after all, but then she decided you'd be safer if she let me go."

"What if she hadn't decided that?" Tom asked.

"Your mother is a cool and intelligent woman, Tom. If she weren't, I would have stolen someone else's children."

"And then you left?" Sharon said.

"I got up, and she asked me if I would have you write her a letter saying that you're well and that you understand you'll be free to go home on September 15. I told her I had planned to have you do that in any case."

"Then what?" Tom asked.

"I checked out of the Plaza and went up the street and checked into the Hampshire House. Then I went for a walk in Central Park and watched the seals in the zoo. That night I went to see a revival of Shaw's play *Candida,* Tuesday morning I went to the Metropolitan Museum, and then I started for home."

"We're glad you're back," Tom said.

"I believe you are," she said.

"Won't the police be after you now?" Tom asked her, enjoying the idea that he was having tea with a fugitive.

"I'm sure they're searching my Vermont farmhouse, which used to belong to your mother's family, you know, right now. But they won't find any clues because I haven't been inside it for ten years. They'll go to the Northfield post office, and the postmaster will tell them that a sweet old lady named Standish rents a box there and comes by every few months wearing the same old print dress to pick up her mail. And that's all he'll have to tell. Everyone in town will act upset, but really be delighted with the excitement, and a lot of them will say that they knew all along that I wasn't what I seemed. That silly picture you have of me will be printed in the newspapers, and still no one will know anything." Aunt Eve shook her head easily and smiled. "Everyone's going to be terribly puzzled," she said.

They were quiet for a minute or so, and then Tom said, "Do you really have a drug that will keep people alive forever?"

Aunt Eve turned toward Mr. Hill.

"You can never tell if something will go on forever," he said, "because you have to wait until the end of forever to find out, and the end of forever never comes. All I can say is that in November 1866 I found a substance which appears to stop most of the changes in the human body for a long time. How long, I don't know, but there's every reason to believe that if you and Sharon begin taking this substance you will remain just as you are now for two or three hundred years at least."

"What's it look like?" Tom asked.

"A big aspirin tablet. If you don't like swallowing pills you can crush it up in applesauce or anything else. It doesn't taste very good, but it's not unpleasant-tasting either."

"And as long as we take these tablets, we can't die, or at least not for a long time?" Sharon asked.

"No, you can still die," he said. "You can fall on the street and break your skull, you can fall off the dock and drown, you can be struck by lightning—lots of things can happen. But if nothing accidental like that happens, a hundred years from now you'll be exactly what you are now."

"Does everyone here take them?" Tom asked.

"Everyone but you and Sharon," he said. He took two brown pill bottles out of his pocket and put them on the coffee table. Then he got up, went to the front window, and gazed out at the street. Perhaps he wanted Aunt Eve to take up the conversation, but she didn't. She was knitting a girl's winter sweater, light red with white snowflakes across the front.

"When did everybody get here?" Tom asked, partly to break the silence.

"Your Aunt Eve came in 1867. I was in Richmond and found out accidentally from a friend that she was alive and well, though her two sons and her husband had been killed in the closing months of the war. I went to see her—I'm sure she thought I had come to court her—and persuaded her to come here with me and help me start a community of good people."

He came back from the window and looked at Tom and Sharon. When he spoke again, there was a special excitement in his voice. "I wanted to gather together a community of people who had already lived good lives, and give them a chance to build a paradise on earth . . . Does that sound silly to you? Childish? . . . It didn't sound silly to me at the time. It still doesn't."

"But I guess it didn't work out the way you wanted it to," Tom said.

"No, it didn't, Tom. Although with you two here now, things may change for the better. Through you, we might all begin to see the world fresh again. Now most of us are like mummies that move. You might change us back into people."

Aunt Eve looked up from her knitting. "It's time for you to write your letter home. Dinner will be ready in a little while, and you remember Mr. Eliot and some friends of his are coming to see us."

"Do you want us to be there when they come?" Sharon asked.

"Yes," she said, and took up her knitting again.

Tom and Sharon left.

When they got upstairs, they decided he'd write the letter, she'd change it, he'd look it over to see

if her changes were all right, and then she'd look it
over one more time to make final corrections. Tom
wrote:

> Dear Dad and Mom,
>   We are well, and hope you are both feeling
> fine and not worrying too much about us. We
> have not been hurt at all, and we are sure we will
> be able to come home on September 15, and look
> forward to coming home then. Please don't
> worry. We love you.
>
> > Love,
> > Tom and Sharon

Sharon thought it was too short, but she couldn't
think of anything to add. After reading it again, she
added "lots of" to the second "love." But that made
the letter end with "We love you. Lots of love,"
which sounded silly. So, after thinking about it for
a few minutes, she crossed out the "Lots of." Then
she suggested that "harmed" be substituted for "hurt,"
and Tom said O.K., but then she changed her mind
again and "hurt" stayed in.

After Tom had copied it and folded it and put it
in an envelope, Sharon took it out again and wrote
across the bottom,

> P.S. I hope you'll be able to do lots of things to-
> gether while we're away. Love, Sharon.

Aunt Eve called them for dinner just as she was
handing the letter back to him.

Before they went downstairs, he took the sketch of his getaway raft out from under the linoleum in his closet and put it in his pocket. He had decided to show it to Aunt Eve.

They were halfway through dinner when he took the sketch out and, without saying anything, put it next to her plate. She stopped eating and looked at it.

"Building a raft to go to sea in is a hard job," she said after looking at it longer than he had expected her to. "Do you want to get home badly enough to try to cut, drag, and bind logs that big?"

Tom didn't know how to answer her question, so he asked one. "Do you really think it would be too much work if Sharon and I did it together?"

"Nothing is too much work if you're completely committed to it and willing to risk your lives. Are you?"

"Sharon doesn't even know about the raft," he said, hoping at least to get her off the hook.

"A boy could injure himself trying to build something that big and heavy. It would be almost too much for a grown man."

"May I see it?" Mr. Hill asked. He got up and came around the table and looked over Aunt Eve's shoulder. "Building a raft is a hard, complicated job," he said, and went back to his end of the table and sat down again. Aunt Eve handed the picture back to Tom, who put it face down next to his plate.

"It's interesting. I appreciate your showing it to me," she said.

"I drew it mostly for fun," Tom said.

"No, you didn't," she said in a calm, easy way. "You did it because you felt that you ought to do it —that you had a moral duty to plan an escape." Tom didn't answer.

"Important problems never have solutions you can draw pictures of, Tom."

Sharon wanted to help him out, so she tried to change the subject. "I read *The Boston Recorder* Monday afternoon, Aunt Eve."

"It was a good newspaper," Aunt Eve said, without taking her eyes off Tom. "Better than most."

"It sure was," Sharon said, but she couldn't think of anything else to say.

"Let's do the dishes and go out for a walk," Mr. Hill said. Everyone but Aunt Eve started to get up.

"I'm almost sure you wouldn't do it, Tom, but if I discovered that you were secretly building a raft, I'd have kerosene poured on it and have it set afire, and lock you in for a week. Blow out the candles, will you, please?"

They got up, washed the dishes, took a walk, came back, and sat together in the living room waiting for Mr. Eliot and his friends. After a while there was a knock on the door. "See who that is, will you, Tom, and don't forget to take their hats and coats."

He started out of the room, and then he stopped

and turned around. "I've been thinking about that raft, Aunt Eve. I think I could build it alone, and I think I could keep it hidden from you, too, if I wanted to."

"You're welcome to try," she said as he went the rest of the way to the door.

The Peace Delegation

Three people were standing outside the door when Tom opened it, Mr. Eliot, Mrs. Balfour, and Mr. Rice, looking naked without his camera. They came in. Tom took Mrs. Balfour's coat from Mr. Eliot, who had taken it from Mr. Rice, who had taken it from Mrs. Balfour, hung it up, and followed them into the living room. Mrs. Balfour sat on the piano bench, as she had on Saturday afternoon, and again she held her handbag tightly between her knees.

Saturday she had worn a pink suit. Now she wore a purple one.

"I assume that you desire the children here while we confer," Mr. Eliot said, placing himself in front of the fireplace, with one foot slightly in front of the other, his left hand resting lightly on the mantlepiece. "Mrs. Balfour, Mr. Rice, and I find that arrangement quite acceptable." Mrs. Balfour looked displeased, Mr. Rice looked uncomfortable, and Mr. Eliot looked anxious to go on. "I want to say, first of all, that we are here as a peace delegation."

"I'm delighted," Aunt Eve said. Mr. Eliot nodded and continued his speech. First he spoke in praise of the glorious past, which he called "that golden time when everyone had a secure sense of his place in the world." Then he praised childhood, which he called "that golden time when every day is a promise and every innocent sleep an invitation to wonderland." Then he praised discipline and stern self-control, which he called "the golden means whereby tranquillity is brought to the commerce between men." All this took him quite a while, and toward the end Tom thought Mrs. Balfour might go to sleep and fall off the piano bench. Unfortunately, she didn't.

Finally, Mr. Eliot got to the point. "No doubt the children have told you," he said, "that while you were away they went to the east shore and started a large, dangerous bonfire. No doubt they have also told you that they went out after their proper bedtime on Monday evening, walked boldly into the village, and invaded my office, leaving behind much clear evidence of their intrusion."

"Burnt matches, cigarettes, and wicked magazines?" Aunt Eve asked with a serious face.

"Unclean footprints," Mr. Eliot said, making Tom wonder for a moment what a clean footprint might be.

"Furthermore," Mrs. Balfour said, coming awake, "they might have knocked me down, they were playing so recklessly in the street—and in the middle of a rainstorm—on Sunday afternoon. Fortunately, I was careful enough to avoid them."

Tom and Sharon looked at each other. They hadn't even seen Mrs. Balfour since the tea, and they wondered if they could both have run by her on Sunday without noticing her. It was, after all, possible. Mr. Hill saw the puzzlement in their faces. "When did the children almost knock you down?" he asked her.

"I didn't say they 'almost' knocked me down, Mr. Hill. I said they 'might' have knocked me down, the wild way they were playing in the rain Sunday. Fortunately for the safety of my life, I remained in the house all day and never went out. Either one of these children could have knocked me down and killed me if I had ventured outside for as much as a moment."

"What do you suggest we do, Mr. Eliot?" Aunt Eve asked in an unhurried way.

"Actually, something very simple and, I'm sure, very agreeable to everyone concerned. We suggest that you surround your back yard with a stout, high, and attractive fence, thereby providing the children with a safe, secluded area of their own. We could put in a sandbox, swings, a slide, perhaps even a little playhouse for them. We're sure that they would quickly learn to enjoy playing there much more than they enjoy going off together to the beach, starting fires, knocking people down on the street, tramping through the woods, and breaking into private property. Clearly, a fenced area for them to play in is the ideal solution." Mr. Eliot smiled at Aunt Eve and Mr. Hill, who looked as calm as monks playing checkers.

"We are not, of course, proposing at this time that the children never be allowed out of their play area. Obviously, if they are closely supervised by two or more adults, there is no reason why they might not be allowed out for walks occasionally, provided that proper warning is posted beforehand. Perhaps a schedule of their outings could be published in the *Islander*. Moreover, we think that such social events as the tea you gave so ably and well on Saturday are excellent from the point of view of their educational value. They could be arranged periodically."

"Is that your entire proposal?" Aunt Eve asked.

"In essence, yes," he said. He looked at Sharon and winked, as if he were helping her put something over on Aunt Eve. "Of course, this is just one proposed solution to the problem the children—of whom, let me say right now, I'm personally very fond—the problem, as I say, which they present. Other solutions along the same lines are no doubt possible."

"Exactly what problem do the children present?" Aunt Eve asked.

"Unpredictability," he said. "They present the problem of unpredictability. Their behavior is unpredictable. It threatens our tranquillity."

"I see," Aunt Eve said as she turned toward Mrs. Balfour. "Would you care for a piece of lemon pie?" Mrs. Balfour was tempted to say yes, because lemon pie was her favorite. Her brother disliked it, so she couldn't make it at home very often for fear that he would begin to think that she disliked him. Her mouth watered. Then she remembered that she was part of a serious delegation. Serious delegates, she felt, don't eat pie. Still, Aunt Eve did make exquisite pies. But, again on the other hand, Mr. Eliot might be upset if she said yes. That decided her. She said yes. Mr. Rice said yes, please, because it would give him something to stare at and play with. Mr. Eliot, not to be alone, agreed to have some, too. So Aunt Eve went out to the kitchen and a few minutes later all three guests had plates to balance and meringue to stab. Then Aunt Eve began to speak.

"I read your editorial very carefully, Mr. Eliot. It's badly written, wordy. You used to write much better than you do now."

Mr. Eliot opened his mouth, but nothing came out.

"None of us seems to care about simplicity any more. We have six or seven people on the island who do nothing but paint pictures, and the pictures are all clumsy and silly. You do engraving, but the best that can be said about it is that your dollar bills look exactly like the United States Treasury's dollar bills, and that, after all, isn't art."

"I did not come here to be insulted," Mr. Eliot said, standing as tall as he could.

"That's a thoughtless answer," Aunt Eve said. "We both know why you came here. You came here because Tom and Sharon frighten you."

"I am not frightened," he said, his voice pitched a little higher.

"But you are frightened. You're frightened for your life. And I'm ashamed for you." She turned to Tom and Sharon. "Mr. Eliot edited an anti-slavery newspaper in western Virginia right up until the beginning of the war, when they put him out of business. It was a good newspaper." She looked back at him. "You had courage, then, and you wrote clearly and honestly. Now you're as dull as most of the rest of us."

Mrs. Balfour stood up as if she were balancing something on her head. "I'm going home," she said. "And I know I'll be safe on my way because these two are indoors where they belong, though they ought to be in bed, instead of menacing innocent people on the streets." It was clear from the way she walked out that she was enormously proud of this speech. She got her coat out of the closet with slow dignity, and was careful not to slam the door behind her.

"You should have gotten her coat, Tom," Aunt Eve said.

"I didn't know she was going till she went," Tom said.

"Maybe I better go too," Mr. Rice said, half getting up and then hanging between standing and sitting.

"We'd be happy to have you stay," Aunt Eve said. "Perhaps Sharon will pass you another piece of pie." She did. He sat down again.

"And now look what's happened," Aunt Eve went on, never taking her eyes from Mr. Eliot. "Half of our people are frightened to death of slipping on the rocks or getting bumped into on the street. Mr. Hill goes off the island and nobody sleeps for fear until he gets back. We bring two children here and you want to put them in a cage. Robert, I'm ashamed for you."

A stillness fell upon the room. In her mind Sharon could hear a clock ticking. Finally Mr. Eliot spoke. "What you say is all very well, Eve, but it doesn't solve our problem."

"You still see the children as a threat, don't you? And they aren't. They're our hope." She paused, and when she spoke again, she was no longer pleading, she was instructing.

"Robert," she said, "I want you to listen to me and understand what I'm saying. I'm going to let these children go home if they want to on September 15. We have until then to help them to want to stay."

Tom and Sharon could see from his expression that he was more than surprised. He was shocked. "That's impossible," he said. "If they went back and told about us, the whole world would come down on us."

"That's right," Aunt Eve said. "*If* they went back, and *if* they told about us, the life we live here now would be over."

"Then it's impossible," he said again. "You can't let them go."

"No, it's not impossible, Robert, you have to understand that. And during these next two and a half months they've got to be given complete freedom. Love and good sense require it."

Mr. Eliot shook his head slowly back and forth a few times. "If they go back, they're bound to tell," he said.

"No, they're not bound to tell, and I don't think they would tell. They're people, Robert, not animals in a zoo. They can be as reasonable and as honorable and as kind as you were once."

Mr. Eliot thought. At least it looked as if he was thinking. Then, without looking up, he said, "I apologize."

"That's the first human thing I've heard you say in a long time, Robert." She got up, took their letter off the mantelpiece, and gave it to him. "Tom and Sharon wrote this to their parents and it has to be mailed. You haven't been back in the world for a long time, and I'd be grateful if you mailed it for

them. Homer's holding the ferry." She took his arm
and walked him slowly to the door. "I suggest you
mail it in St. Louis or some place farther west."

Mr. Rice slid around behind him and got his hand
on the doorknob. He smiled toward Tom. "Come
and see my cameras some day. You can play with
them." Then, tipping a hat that wasn't there, he
squeezed through the door. Mr. Eliot opened it farther. "Good night, and thank you for your hospital-
ity." A moment later he was gone, and the four were
alone again.

"Do you think he'll mail it?" Sharon asked, linger-
ing by the door while the others slowly went back
into the living room. "I'm sure of it," Aunt Eve said.
"He's a better man than I made him appear tonight."

Sharon followed her into the living room with a
doubting look on her face.

"You never see the whole of any character at any
one time, Sharon," Aunt Eve said. "You only see part
of it, and not always the best part. Think of yourself,
for example. Since you came here you've shown more
fear and suspicion than you've ever shown in your
whole life. I'm not blaming you for that—if anyone's
to blame, it's me—I'm only saying that there are
other things in your character that are just as much
a part of you as suspicion and fear are. There's trust,
and courage, and a joy in life. The same thing is true
of Mr. Eliot. There's more to him than selfishness."

Sharon wanted to leave the room. She hated to
have people talk about her character. Tom could

see she was upset, and tried to help by asking a question. "The money Mr. Eliot makes. Why does he do it?"

"I don't know, Tom," Aunt Eve said. "He says he prints money as a hobby. I think he does it because he enjoys the idea of beating the world at its own game. Counterfeiting money makes him feel powerful, and everybody likes to feel powerful, even old ladies and children."

"You mean he never spends it?"

"He doesn't need to," Mr. Hill said. "Every person here put his money into a common fund when he came. It was one of the requirements. We live on the interest, which this year amounted to something under three hundred thousand dollars. What we don't spend, we give away at the end of the year."

Aunt Eve spoke. "It's time you both went to bed."

Mr. Hill handed them the pill bottles. As Sharon took hers, she looked at him. "Do *you* want us to take them?"

"Yes," he said. "I do."

A few minutes later they were both in their pajamas. Without talking about it at all, they each swallowed a tablet. Then they went to bed. Tom went to sleep

right away, but Sharon didn't. After she had been lying awake for a while, Aunt Eve came quietly into
her room and sat down at the foot of her bed.

"Knowing you're going to be free to go on September 15 doesn't make it any easier for you now,
does it?"

Sharon said nothing.

"You're like someone in prison who has just begun
to discover that it isn't such a bad place after all.
The closer his day of release comes, the more he's
torn between wanting to stay and wanting to go.
He might even start planning an escape just to avoid
deciding whether he really wants to go or not."

Sharon still didn't say anything.

"You'll probably put it off for a while, but one day
you'll be alone, watching the sea, and you'll find
yourself choosing the island or the world. Whatever
you decide on that day I'm sure will be right . . .
Good night, Sharon."

She didn't say good night back.

The next morning they found a copy of the
Islander on the dining-room table. It had SPECIAL
WEDNESDAY EDITION written across the top of it, and
running down the middle of the page was an editorial.

MATURE FLEXIBILITY

It is the duty of every human being to treat his
guests kindly and politely. This duty is recog-

nized even in the world. It is a special privilege to be kind and polite when one's guests are such fine people as we had the great privilege of meeting at tea on Saturday past, a fair lass and a well set up young gentleman from the City of New York.

Some persons, including your editor, greeted their arrival politely but without enthusiasm. Honesty compels me to confess to having accompanied my welcome with doubts, yes, almost with hostility. However, it is the function of a mature mind to be flexible, and the function of a humble mind to admit its errors. Therefore, your editor takes the opportunity of this Extra Edition to apologize to our young guests for any lack of warmth he may have displayed toward them, in person or in print, and to apologize to his readers for any indications he might have given them that caution and watchfulness were called for.

On the contrary, we are grateful for the presence of these young guests in our midst, and have recently become convinced of the virtue of their coming *and staying*. Clearly, we should long ago have welcomed two youngsters among us, and we fully expect these belated but heartily welcome guests to remain as part of our permanent citizenry. It should be abundantly clear to all of us that we must bend every effort of action and will toward effecting their *permanent happiness here with us*. Your editor will certainly do his part in this high-minded community endeavor.

At the bottom of the page it said that there would be no Sunday edition, "due to the absence of the Editor on an errand of consequence elsewhere."

"What do you think of Mr. Eliot's editorial?" Aunt Eve asked as she brought in pancakes. Sharon didn't feel like answering questions, especially from Aunt Eve, but she answered anyway. "He doesn't sound very sincere to me." She sat down and drank some of her orange juice.

"Do you think he's being a hundred percent insincere or only ninety-five percent insincere?"

"Ninety-eight percent."

"Then there's a two-percent piece of honesty still left in him," Aunt Eve said with a smile. "Or am I being too generous?"

"I don't know," Sharon said. She stared down at her plate. "You always make things sound the way you want them to sound, as if you were the only one who knew anything, and everything anybody did was just the way you planned for them to do it. Other people can be right sometimes too, not just you."

She got up, knocking her chair off balance, and walked fast out of the room. She was gone before her chair hit the floor. She started up the stairs, changed her mind, came back down, and went out the door. Tom and Aunt Eve sat stiff.

"Do you think I ought to go after her?" he asked.

"You've known her longer than I have," Aunt Eve said. "What do you think?"

"I don't know," he said as he got up from the table and went toward the front door. "I guess I'll see where she's going." He didn't really want to catch up with her, he just wanted to get out of the house, see that she was all right, and be by himself. When he got outside, she was standing in the front yard staring at a yellow rosebud on the big bush under the living-room window.

"You looking for something?"

"I'm just looking . . . I don't want to stand out here and have people see me just standing out here doing nothing."

"Oh."

"What do you mean, 'Oh'?"

"I don't know . . . Nothing special."

"Well, I wish people wouldn't say things like that and not know what they mean," she said, still staring at the rosebud.

"Tom," she said after a while, "do you think I'm vain and selfish?" Tom knew instantly that she had read Mr. Hill's last letter about her.

"Well, do you?" she asked again.

"No," he said, caring much more how his voice sounded than how true his answer was.

"No, tell the truth," she said, studying the unfinished flower more and more intently. "Mr. Hill said I was, in one of his letters about me. If Aunt Eve said it I wouldn't care, but if he says it I think maybe it's true." She stopped staring at the bud and started walking slowly toward the street. When she got there, she turned left, away from the village. Tom walked with her.

"Once in a while you might act so that people who didn't really know you might think you were that way, but you aren't."

"Well, if I act selfish I must be selfish," she said, trying to sound cool and detached about it.

"You can be a lot of things at the same time," Tom said, "not just one thing." He realized that he was saying exactly what Aunt Eve had said the night before, and hoped she wouldn't notice. "Sometimes I'm mean," he said, "but I'm not all mean."

"You sound just like Aunt Eve," she said. "I know I'm not beautiful. I don't think I'm beautiful just because I've got a nice dress on. I wish I didn't have any nice dresses at all."

"Well, I think you're beautiful," he said. He didn't expect that to help, and it didn't.

"You don't know what you're talking about," she said. "It's not your fault, but you just don't understand."

"See, you're being nice to me now," Tom said. "I think you're wonderful, really, I couldn't ask for a better sister. Remember once how I wrote you you were better than a brother? Well, you are, really, I mean it, you are."

"But you think I'm vain and selfish too," she said, and Tom knew that whatever answer he gave would only make things worse, so he didn't say anything. A man was coming toward them along the road. He passed them and then he stopped and called to them, so they had to turn around.

"Good morning. Out for a morning walk, I see. I'm Mr. Jordan. I live in the house on the left, beyond those elm trees."

Tom and Sharon smiled and said good morning. "Well," Mr. Jordan said, "I hope you have a healthy morning." He turned toward the village and moved on.

"Why don't you go back to the house," Sharon said as they watched Mr. Jordan walking away like a careful duck.

"I'd just as soon be here with you," he said.

"I wish you would, anyway," Sharon said. "I'll be all right, and I'd like to be alone for a little while."

"O.K.," he said. "Then I'll see you around lunch. You're sure there's nothing I can do for you?"

"No, really, I don't need anything," she said, and turning, she walked on down the road. She didn't look back.

As she walked, she got more and more angry at Aunt Eve, at Tom, at the island, at the world, and at herself. She had taken one of the tablets. She, Sharon Inlander, a prisoner, had taken one of the tablets. She really should have thrown them in the fire or flushed them down the toilet, and she had taken one. She should have put big holes in Mrs.

Balfour's coat pockets or pulled all the buds off Aunt Eve's rosebushes. She was a prisoner, she and Tom both, and they were acting like sweet, obedient children.

But no more, not any more. They'd build a raft after all. And the night they left in it, they'd sneak into Aunt Eve's room first and quickly tie her wrists and ankles to the bedposts. Then they'd tell her they were going. And she'd just lie there trying to get loose and not being able to, even though she was strong, because they'd tied her so tight with Boy Scout knots. And they'd gag her too, so she wouldn't have a chance to say anything. She'd just lie there, struggling, with her eyes popping and her hair all loose. And then they'd back slowly out of the room, looking at her with calm, strong faces.

What a victory that would be.

She noticed something red next to the road. She walked up close to it and leaned over. It was a wild strawberry. It looked exactly like the strawberries that came to the store in boxes, only smaller. "Good," she thought to herself, "we won't have to take any of her food." She could already start gathering strawberries and drying them in the sun the way they dry grapes in California, and then they'd have plenty of food for the trip. Hidden behind a low bush she found a rock that was flat on top. She began picking strawberries and laying them in rows on the rock. The work went slowly. Some of the strawberries were tiny, and they were all small. Her wrists and neck began to itch, and her back was soaked with sweat.

After she had laid out five rows of ten strawberries each, she began to wonder if they really would dry like raisins. They might just rot. She decided to eat all but one row and come back every day and watch what happened. Then, if they did become strawberry-raisins, she could gather and dry a lot of them. When she was through eating the four rows, she realized that she was hungry.

She decided to have lunch with Mr. Hill. Let Aunt Eve worry about her if she wanted to. It would do her good to worry. She wiped her face on her sleeve and jumped the five or six steps back to the road. When she got back to the road, she noticed that her ankles had lots of tiny cuts on them, which didn't bother her at all. She was rather proud of them.

As she walked, it came to her that maybe Mr. Hill might also secretly want to escape, that he might just be waiting for her to come and talk to him about breaking back into the world, and that the two of them together might work out a bold, clever, complicated, and foolproof way of doing it.

After three minutes of enjoying this idea, she realized that she was being foolish. Mr. Hill certainly didn't hate Aunt Eve, and certainly wouldn't help her escape. Which was all right because the raft really had no room for adults, anyway. She began to think about how surprised and worried Aunt Eve would be when she didn't come home for lunch. She'd show her that she really didn't need her. She'd teach her she wasn't so powerful. She began to feel stronger, and hungrier, and walked a little faster toward Mr. Hill's house.

xiv

Feeling Two Ways at Once

She met Tom on the way back. He had been worrying about her, but he didn't want to tell her. "I thought you might forget," he said, "so I thought I'd come and tell you it's almost time for lunch."

"I'm eating at Mr. Hill's house," Sharon said as if she had already been invited.

"What if he's at the drugstore?"

"Then I'll eat with him there." She began to walk a little faster. "What have you been doing?"

"Just walking around."

He didn't ask any more questions, but just walked along beside her.

"You go on home," she said when they got to Mr. Hill's house.

"You want me to tell Aunt Eve you're here?"

"If you want to tell her, you can, and if you don't, don't. It doesn't make any difference to me." She walked up the stone path to Mr. Hill's front door and knocked. "Come in," he called from the back of the house. "It's open." Without looking back at Tom, whom she could feel watching her from the street, she opened the door and went inside.

"Who is it?"

"It's me."

"Tom with you?"

"No, it's just me."

"Come on in the kitchen. Would you like some lunch?"

"Thank you."

"Does everyone know where you are?"

"Tom does, and he's going to tell Aunt Eve."

"Good. Come sit down at the table. The soup's just about done."

They ate. After ice cream, they got up and washed the dishes and then went out onto the small back porch. Mr. Hill sat down on the top step. Sharon sat down next to him.

"What's on your mind?"

"I don't know."

"Oh."

"Right now I'm thinking about Aunt Eve, I guess."

"She's been doing a lot of thinking about you, too. She came over right after breakfast this morning and we talked about you. Not just about you, we talked about Tom too, but mostly about you. She had decided to send you two home today."

Sharon's heart missed a beat, and she blushed. She found she didn't want to be sent home right away. Tomorrow maybe, but not this afternoon. "Oh," she said.

"She knows this is a hard time for you, and even harder for your parents, and she feels the whole responsibility for it." Mr. Hill paused, and then he went on: "I talked her out of it, Sharon, because I think it's important for you two to be here."

"Oh."

"Look what's happened already because you're here. Mr. Eliot has admitted, on the front page of his own newspaper, that he was wrong. Mrs. Balfour, who in the past fifty years has become a mean old lady, came to ask me this morning what your favorite cake is, so she could bake it for you. By the way, what is your favorite cake?"

"Chocolate."

"Do you mind if I tell her?"

"No, I don't mind." Sharon imagined her bedroom running over with chocolate cakes from Mrs. Balfour's busy-twenty-four-hours-a-day-oven.

"Of course, they're starting to be nice to you now

because they're afraid you'll go back and tell the world about the island. Nevertheless, they *are* beginning to do a few new things, to break old habits, to see beyond their own front doors. As long as you're here, everyone, including your Aunt Eve and I, is going to be acting like a better person. And if you're here long enough, maybe we'll become better people. You two have started a reformation."

"Is that what you want, really?"

"Yes. Why?"

"Because if you want things to change, then I don't understand what you meant about Mr. Simpson. You told us you were glad he didn't ever get any smarter, because you wanted things to stay the same."

"That's right, I do."

"How can you want Tom and me to change things, and at the same time want everything to stay the same?"

"Because I'm a human being, Sharon, and like most human beings, I want things to stay exactly the way they are, because I'm afraid that otherwise they might get worse, and at the same time I want things to change, because I'm sick to death of living through the same old thing over and over again. I'm like you. You want to stay here, and at the same time you want to go home. You want us to send you back, and you want us to hold you.

"Tom feels the same way, too, I'm sure. You two are a lot alike, you know. You both want to be loved, and you're both able to love." He looked directly at her.

"The difference is that it's harder for you to love than
it is for him. His heart makes connections quicker
than yours does. That's one reason why you're feeling
so mixed up now, because your love has to go somewhere and it doesn't yet know where to go, or how."

Sharon turned her eyes from Mr. Hill and looked
out at his garden. She looked at his flowers, and relaxed, and began to feel peaceful. He was right. He
had told her the truth.

She wanted to kiss him.

She kept watching the flowers for a while, not
saying anything. Mr. Hill was silent, too. Finally she
asked a question. She asked it lightly, easily, but she
knew it wasn't a light, easy question.

"Do you really think that what you're doing is
right?"

"Ask me again on September 15, after you've made
your decision about staying or going." He got up and
went inside. A minute later he came out with a
checkerboard and some checkers. He sat down on
the top step again. "It's time you gave me a lesson in
how to play." They started to lay the checkers out.

Meanwhile, back at strawberry-raisin rock, a big
robin and his wife were finishing a delicious lunch.

xv

Reconciliation

Sharon arrived back at Aunt Eve's just in time for dinner, and as she was putting salt on her mashed potatoes, she said to her, "Can you read some more of *The Swiss Family Robinson* tonight?"

"Good idea," Aunt Eve said, and things were all right between them again. The words of reconciliation had been spoken.

After dinner they took a walk through the village and down to the shore. On their way there, one old man and two old women smiled at them in a super-friendly way. They looked at the water for a while, Tom and Sharon picked up a few shells, and they walked back home. Tom made a fire and Aunt Eve read three chapters of *The Swiss Family Robinson*. The last light was just going out of the sky when they got on their pajamas, took their tablets, and went to bed.

July

July was a hot, happy month. The sunny days were great, and the rainy days were just as good. Aunt Eve got through *The Swiss Family Robinson* and then read them a wonderful book by T. H. White, *Mistress Masham's Repose*. Everyone on the island seemed livelier, and Tom and Sharon knew that they were the cause of it. The only boring day of the week was Sunday, when Mr. Eliot came to dinner, and that wasn't too bad except when he read aloud what he was writing for the *Islander*.

One long article about his visit to St. Louis ended, "I plan to go abroad again in the fall, this time to Chicago." He imagined himself quite an adventurer.

They built a fort in the woods behind Mr. Hill's house and stocked it with the jars of cookies and candies and fruit people kept giving them. They found climbing trees. They swam. They watched sunrises and sunsets. Sometimes, at night, they'd take long walks with Aunt Eve and Mr. Hill. Then, when they got tired, they'd sit down together, and Tom would build a fire, and they'd sing, or talk, or just be quiet.

On especially beautiful nights Tom and Sharon would leave them by the fire and go off alone, exploring the dark beach and watching the white breakers come in under the moonlit clouds. Often, Aunt Eve and Mr. Hill would go home ahead of them, and when they got home there would be cocoa ready in the kitchen. Then they'd drag themselves happily off to bed.

Aunt Eve and Mr. Hill were always there when they wanted them, but never got in the way. The four became intimate friends.

Every day in July was good except for one, the last day, which was scary. Tom woke up very early and started to throw up. He felt sicker than he had ever felt before in his life. Mr. Hill came and examined him carefully, pushing and poking and listening and asking questions. Tom, with nausea sitting on the back of his tongue, was sure it was the tablets that had made him sick. So was Sharon. Mr. Hill didn't say anything or leave any medicine, and Tom could tell from his eyes that he was worried. He said he'd come back in the middle of the afternoon. Tom hated to see him leave.

Sharon stayed with him all morning so he wouldn't be lonely. Around noon he began to feel better, but not much. He fell asleep and had confusing dreams. It was late afternoon when Mr. Hill gently woke him up. "Mr. Rice is throwing up, too, and I don't feel so well myself," he said, smiling. "Mr. Eliot must have brought a virus back with him from St. Louis." Tom relaxed. "So it wasn't the tablets that did it," Mr. Hill said, as Tom lay thinking the same thing in the same words.

"Where's Sharon?" Tom asked. "Did you tell her?"

"We told her," he said. "She's in taking a bath now, I think." Suddenly Tom was completely awake and feeling fine. He was also very hungry. "Can I have something to eat?" Mr. Hill turned around, and Tom saw Aunt Eve standing behind him. "What would you like?" she asked.

"Cinnamon buns and cocoa with marshmallows in it."

She smiled and shook her head. "Toast and strawberry jam and tea," she said, and that sounded good to him, too. She went downstairs and brought it back in almost no time, and then she and Mr. Hill went downstairs again.

Sharon came in a few minutes later. "How do you feel now?" she said, sitting down on the end of his bed.

"Good."

"That was scary, wasn't it?"

"A little." They were silent awhile.

"Tom?" Sharon stopped, and Tom didn't answer. "Tom, have you felt any different this month?"

"No, I don't think so. You?"

"No. But, you know the second day we took the tablets? Well, I measured myself against my closet door, and then I measured myself again just now to see if I'd really stopped growing."

"Did you?"

"I think so. In fact, I think maybe I even shrunk a little. Not very much, just a little bit."

"That couldn't happen," Tom said. "I haven't noticed you getting any smaller."

"It's not so much that anybody'd notice it," she said. "Anyway, I'm going to measure myself again in September and see."

"Let me see where you did it," Tom said, and got right out of bed. They went quietly into her room, shut the door, and walked slowly over to the closet. Inside the closet door there were two tiny pencil marks you could hardly see unless you were looking for them and knew how high to look.

"Stand the way you were and I'll measure," Tom said. According to his measurement she had grown an inch.

"You're not doing it right," she said.

"Yes, I am. Nobody can really do it for himself because you always have to work behind your own back."

"That doesn't make any difference," she said. "I did it the same way both times."

"I'll do it for you again in September," Tom said, "and then we'll know for sure." He walked slowly across the room and lay down across her bed. He felt just a little bit dizzy.

"You feel all right?" Sharon asked.

"Sure." He shut his eyes and tried to relax.

"What do you think we ought to do?" she asked after a little while. "Do you think we ought to stay here?"

"We can't," Tom said, keeping his eyes closed and trying to sound sure of himself. "We can't leave Dad and Mom worrying about us forever. It just wouldn't be fair."

"I guess you're right," she said.

"*You* want to go, don't you?" he said, opening his eyes.

"Sure I do," she said. "I know we can't stay here forever."

"The only thing we might do," Tom said, "if we really wanted to and thought it would really be a good idea, would be to stay here a year, maybe until next September. If we're really doing some good here, we might do that. It wouldn't be as if we were wasting a year out of our lives. I mean next summer we'll still be the same age we are now. But I wouldn't want to do it unless you wanted to do it."

"We might do that," Sharon said, trying to sound detached and wise.

"I could write them another letter," Tom said—he was beginning to feel better again—"and you could look at it to see if it was all right, like we did before, and we could tell them that we're doing something important, that we're well, and everything like that, and that we've decided to spend almost exactly a year here altogether before we come home."

"Shall we do it?" Sharon asked, quite excited but trying to keep the excitement out of her voice. "I've never been on an island in the winter."

"If it's all right with you," Tom said. "I think it's a pretty good idea."

"You don't mind staying the same age for a year?"

"No, I don't mind. I like being my age. I'm in no hurry. And if we change our minds any time, we can always go home." Tom put out his hand toward her. "Let's shake on it."

They shook hands.

"But let's not tell Aunt Eve yet," Sharon said.

"You think we might change our minds?"

"No, it's just that she said we should decide on September 15, so I think we should tell her then.

Maybe she doesn't want to know till then, or doesn't want us to make up our minds so soon."

"O.K."

Tom got up, said good night, and went to bed feeling a little dizzy. Then he got out of bed, went into the bathroom, took his tablet, and went back to bed again.

August

All through July, Tom and Sharon had been getting used to the idea of staying on the island, but it wasn't until they had talked about it and shaken hands on it that they began to realize what staying meant. Now, as early August came and went, they both began to feel terribly far away from the world. They even began to feel far away from each other.

The next morning, Tom still felt a little weak. Aunt Eve brought him breakfast in bed, and he spent most of the day sleeping and looking out the window. The day after that, he felt almost completely well again. The morning was gray and chilly and damp, but he and Sharon wanted to go out. Sharon had stayed in the house all the time Tom was sick. To keep Aunt Eve from worrying about them being caught in the rain, they took along their raincoats and rain hats. It didn't rain, and they came home earlier than they had expected to, after spending half the day being bored and looking for something to do.

July had been the happiest month ever. August became the unhappiest month ever. In the first half of it, they did all the things they had done in July, and more. They improved their fort, they picked raspberries, they planned a tree house, and they went to the movies. *Goodbye Broadway, Hello Arizona!* was still playing, and after seeing it every day for a week, they decided it was the funniest movie in the world. Mr. Fleisher, who ran the theater, offered to get a different movie for them, but they told him they liked watching the one he already had. Going to *Goodbye Broadway, Hello Arizona!* was the only thing they didn't get tired of doing. The happiest moments they had that month were the moments they spent sitting alone in the darkened theater giggling and shouting at the screen.

They went on picnics—with Aunt Eve, with Mr. Hill, with Aunt Eve and Mr. Hill, and alone together. They went for walks. Sharon started a diary, and kept it up for three days. Tom started to build a model boat, quit, and then finished it in one busy afternoon of sloppy work. That night, after everyone else was asleep, he went to the beach and burned it. Burning it was the only part he really enjoyed. They gave names to everything—trees, hills, rocks, coves— and then spent one afternoon writing down all the names they could remember and then changing them. When they'd renamed everything, they tore the list in little pieces and threw it in the ocean.

Every day was busy and every day was tiresome. Worst of all, for both of them, they came less and less to enjoy being with each other. They were with each other most of the time, and they never quarreled, but they didn't have any fun together, either, except at the movies. And toward the end of the month they had to force themselves to laugh even there.

Worst of all, they never once in the entire month talked to each other about anything that mattered to either one of them. They even stopped saying good night to each other.

Finally, August was over.

A City and a Crab

One afternoon early in September, Tom and Sharon were lying under their twisted old pine tree on the beach wondering what to do. After a while Tom decided he'd build another sand city, just like the one they'd built together when they first came to the island and Aunt Eve went away to New York. He rolled over on his stomach and tried to get back the feeling he had had then. After a while Sharon got up.

"I guess I'll walk down the beach a little way," she said.

"What are you going to do?"

"Nothing much. You want to come?"

"No, I'm going to build a city. You want to stay and work on it with me?"

"No, I think I'll just walk around a little bit." She started away, and Tom noticed that she was wearing her bathing suit. "You aren't going swimming, are you?" he asked.

"I don't know," she said, still walking away. She stopped and picked up a sweat shirt she had left on the beach a week or ten days before, shook the sand out of it, and began walking again.

"Well, be careful," Tom called after her. She said something back, but he couldn't understand what it was. He felt he really should get up and go after her, but he didn't want to. To take his mind off imagining her drowning, he got up and set to work on the city.

He decided to build it exactly where he and Sharon had built the other one. He went and got some driftwood boards like the one they had used then, except that these boards were heavier, and he worked hard building up the outside walls, glancing up every few minutes to see how close the tide was coming. Then he built the big square main building and put roads around it. He couldn't remember whether Sharon had called it the Town Hall or the City Hall, and that bothered him.

He worked on the roads, paving them very carefully with stones, and then he built four small houses with beach grass roofs, just as Sharon had done. Then he remembered that they had had watchtowers at the ends of the front wall, so he added them, putting flagpoles on top. He stepped back and looked at his work. It looked exactly like the old city, except that the old one had looked alive, and this one looked dead.

He had a long wait before the first wave of the incoming tide hit it, taking away part of the front wall. A moment later he was hard at work repairing the wall, and he kept working against the tide until the city had fallen and his shirt and pants were soaked.

He washed his hands and arms in the salt water, and went back to his tree, and sat down, and wondered why it hadn't been any fun building and trying to save this city. He thought of the original city, and then he thought of all the other cities he and his family had built during vacations on Cape Cod. They were all fun. Some were more fun than others, but they were all fun. Now the special excitement of building a city against the tide was gone. It wasn't any fun any more. Why?

Why?

It was a frightening question, and he didn't want to answer it. Then he remembered something his father had told him once: "When you become afraid of a question, be glad, because you're about to discover something new."

"What if you can't find the answer, or if there isn't any?" Tom had asked him.

"Then at least you'll understand your question better," his father had told him, "and the more you know, even about your questions, the less you have to be afraid of."

Tom believed his father, so he took a deep breath, as he sat under his tree, and he said out loud to the ocean, "Why isn't life fun any more?" The answer came like a wave, and when it came, he realized that he had already known it for weeks. "Because I'm taking the tablets and my life is standing still."

Tom suddenly saw clearly that part of the fun of playing is knowing that the next time you play, things will be different, knowing that this kickball game, or this game of tag, or this game of football, can never happen just this way again, because the people throwing and kicking and running are at the same time growing and changing. The rules may not change, but the players will.

For Tom, now, there were no changes. Tomorrow he and everyone on the island would be the same people they were today. Next summer's weather might be different, but next summer's Tom would be the same —no change, no growth, no decay, no gain, no loss, nothing done that could not be undone, nothing left undone which couldn't just as well be done later. No risks, no limits, no hurry, no hope.

Tom knew that he would never again take one of

the tablets, and the knowledge made him feel free. He stood up and stretched and looked toward the sea. He was surprised to find that the sun was going down. He started to walk fast in the direction Sharon had gone. He had to tell her right away what he had decided.

While Tom was building his city, Sharon was walking. Finally she stopped, and looked at the water, and wondered if she wanted to go in or not. Without deciding yes or no, she dropped her sweat shirt on the sand and walked in. The waves were easy, and the bottom was sandy and smooth, except for a few boulders. She kept on until the water was up to her chest, not trying to swim but just letting herself go up and down with the waves as they came by. After bobbing awhile, she turned around, came out again, and walked on along the beach. A wind began to blow, and she started to shiver. She sat down, hunching her knees up and putting her arms around them.

Next to her there was a board. One end of it was buried in the sand, and the other end was pointing toward the sea. On the board sat a bone-white crab, his shell about the size of a nickel, his claws shorter than Sharon's little finger. He was watching the water, and sniffing it, and listening to it. He was so small, and so complete, that he made her think of a newborn baby.

He moved forward an inch, startling her. Obviously, he wanted to get into the water. He moved forward another inch, stopped, and then moved forward again. Now he had reached the end of the board, and Sharon worried that he might move again and fall off. She pulled together all her courage and put her hand in front of him, palm up, inviting him to climb on.

After a while, her arm began to get tired. Suddenly, lightly, he brushed the edge of her hand with a cool claw. It made her shiver, but she kept her nerve and held her hand still. A minute later, he crawled onto her open palm. Slowly she lifted up the hard-shelled, fragile little child and brought him close to her. He was beautiful.

The tide was coming in and Sharon was glad she was there to save her friend from it. She knew that somewhere out there under the water was a big black greasy fish waiting to suck him up and melt him under his meaty tongue.

The crab began sniffing and listening again, restless. The sweat on her hand seemed to bother him.

He moved, and Sharon's whole body jerked, flipping him out of her hand. He landed hard on his back, flopped over, and started for the water. She pulled the board out of the sand and put it down in front of him to stop him. He stopped. "It's for your own good," she thought to herself. "If you walk into the water, you'll get eaten in no time."

He climbed slowly onto the board, which was just what Sharon had been hoping he'd do. She quickly dragged it a few yards farther back from the water. "I don't want to make a pet out of you," she said to herself. "Really, I just want to help you." But she could see he didn't want her help. He scuttled off the board and started again, in a sideways, sneaky, stop and start kind of way, for the water.

"I'll never save him," Sharon said to herself. He would walk into the ocean, and that big slimy fish would come along and suck him up and not even notice it. Stupid crab. So stupid he was beyond help. Sharon got down on her hands and knees and put her face close to him. He stopped and looked at her. She could tell he was getting mad again. She sat down by him. He didn't move. After a few minutes she thought that maybe, by some miracle, he had seen the light and wouldn't go into the water. She held her breath, waiting to see what he would do, until her chest hurt.

Then he began again to make his way toward the sea, toward death. He was so brave and at the same time so stupid. He came to the place where the wet sand began, and stopped. Suddenly he ran forward a foot and dug himself in.

He was gone. Where she had last seen him, there was just a small hump in the sand, and a wave washed that flat right away. He was gone. She could hardly believe it. Her friend wasn't so stupid after all. The big greasy fish who waited under the water for him wouldn't get him. Not tonight, anyway.

Not knowing why, Sharon felt happier than she'd felt since July. It was a sad kind of happiness, because she longed to see her courageous, clever friend again, and she knew she never would, but it was happiness just the same. She looked down at the spot where she thought she had seen him last. He was gone, and she knew he had completely forgotten her. She closed her eyes tight, and again she could see his perfectly formed body as he stood on the board reaching out toward the sea. She longed to imitate him, to be as courageous and clever as he had been.

And then she knew that it was time to leave the island.

She turned and began to run fast, back along the beach. In a few minutes she saw Tom coming toward her. She waved and tried to run faster. He began running, too. They came up to each other and stopped, out of breath.

"Tom, I want to go home."

"So do I."

They didn't know whether to laugh, or cry, or play tag. They began to walk back toward where their sneakers were. He put his arm on her shoulder, and she put her arm around his waist.

"Where's your sweat shirt?"

"I must have dropped it somewhere on the beach." Her bathing suit was still wet, and the wind was still blowing, but she didn't notice it.

At the pine tree they put on their sneakers and started for Aunt Eve's house. Sharon didn't think of her crab, and Tom didn't think of his city. They just moved along in silence, feeling like brother and sister again.

"I think we should tell her now," Tom said when they were almost there. Sharon nodded.

"Mr. Hill, too."

So they went to his house first and asked him, please, if he didn't have anything special to do, if he'd come over to Aunt Eve's, because they wanted to talk about something.

xix

Trying a Choice

A few minutes later, Tom and Sharon and Aunt Eve and Mr. Hill were sitting together in the living room feeling tense.

Tom looked at Aunt Eve. "We've decided to go home."

"I know."

"We decided alone. We didn't talk to each other about it, we both just decided."

"But you're not really sure yet."

"We're sure."

"No, you're not. If you were, you'd be willing to wait until September 15 to tell us."

"We're sure," Tom said.

"What made you decide?"

"It's hard to say."

"Try."

"It might just sound silly to you."

"It might even sound silly to you," Mr. Hill said, leaning forward.

"Maybe, but even if it did, that wouldn't make it wrong . . . It's because I'm getting so I can't play any more either, like you."

Mr. Hill turned toward Aunt Eve. "It's a strong reason," he said. She looked toward Sharon.

"Your reason isn't the same as Tom's."

"No, it isn't."

"What is it?"

Slowly, carefully, she told Aunt Eve the story of her meeting with the crab. She talked as if Aunt Eve were the only person in the room, and with a seriousness in her voice that Tom had never heard before. "All the crab knew," Sharon said at the end, "was that he was a crab, and that he had to do what crabs are meant to do."

"No, Sharon," Aunt Eve said. "He didn't know anything. He did what he did automatically, by instinct. You're different. You have a mind. You can think. You can choose to live one way or the other."

Sharon answered slowly and deliberately. "Then I

choose to live the way everyone else in the world has to live."

"And you understand that choosing to live like everyone else means choosing to die, in time, too?"

"Yes."

Tom leaned forward. "We understand that," he said.

"I'm sure you do, Tom, a little," Aunt Eve said. She looked back at Sharon. "You're both very young."

"We can't help that," Tom said without anger, and after that they were quiet for a minute or so. Then Sharon said, "I'm who I am, Aunt Eve, and I've got to live like other people."

"It's no virtue to live like 'other people,' Sharon."

"Please, Aunt Eve . . ."

"Please what? Please make it easy for you? No, I'm not going to make it easy for you. This is a whim, a silly whim you got because you lost your pet crab."

"I didn't want to make him a pet."

"You're talking nonsense, Sharon."

"No! It's not that," she said. "It's not!"

She shut her eyes, and immediately she was in Delia Webster's dirty prison cell, suffering with her for helping slaves escape. Delia was sitting in a long dress on a low wooden stool. Her face was serene, and her eyes clear, even in the gray cell. Then, for a moment, Sharon *became* Delia, and in that moment she knew, better than she had ever known anything before, that if she lost her courage now, if she gave in, if she chose to stay out of the world in order to live forever, something in her would die.

When she looked at Aunt Eve again, there was something in her face that showed she was unshakable. She spoke almost in a whisper.

"I don't know as much as you do, Aunt Eve, and I can't argue with you, but I've got to go back and live in the world, and you can talk as much as you want and it won't change me. I have to."

Aunt Eve got up and went out of the room. A few minutes later, she came back with tea. "If you two are leaving tomorrow, we ought to arrange a few things," she said, and began to pour.

"Do you want to tell the islanders yourselves?" Aunt Eve asked, handing Tom a cup of tea.

"How would we do it?"

"Call them all together in the Meeting House, stand up, and say you're leaving. You don't have to do it. You can just leave quietly if you want to. The ferry's in. We could go right now."

"No, we should tell them ourselves," Tom said. "The Meeting House sounds like a good place."

"Then we'll ask Mr. Simpson tonight if we can use it in the morning. If he says yes, we'll be able to leave before noon. We're seventeen miles to sea. It takes about four hours to get across. If we drive all night, we can be in New York early the next morning."

"What do you think they'll say when we tell them?" Tom asked. Aunt Eve thought a few moments. "They'll be surprised, shocked perhaps. Frightened that you'll tell the world all about us."

"We wouldn't," Tom said.

"It will be hard for you not to tell," Mr. Hill said. "Harder than you think now. You might tell things you don't want to tell, just by accident."

"Then we just won't say anything at all," Tom said.

"You can try, anyway, Tom," Mr. Hill said, and then, changing the subject, said to Sharon, "Remember the day you came to have lunch with me and talk?"

She nodded yes.

"You asked me then if I thought I was doing the right thing, keeping all these people alive. I told you I'd answer you on September 15. Since you're not going to be here then, I should try to answer now, and the answer is that I don't know. What I do know is that I've promised these people that they could have the tablets as long as they wanted them, and a promise is a promise. It has to be kept."

Tom and Sharon waited for him to go on, but he didn't.

Aunt Eve spoke. "I know that you two must feel it's been a long time since we came here, but it's really been a very short time. I can remember the first time I sat in this room as if it were yesterday, and all the things that have happened since then look to me now like nothing more than a short sentence in a very long book. In history, every time is close to every other time."

Sharon thought of the wonderful afternoon she had spent with *The Boston Recorder,* and remembered how close the past had seemed to her then, and understood what Aunt Eve meant. She resolved that, like Tom, she would never tell anybody, not even her parents, about these people. She would help Mr. Hill to keep his promise.

She thought ahead to their meeting the next morning with all the islanders. It worried her. "Maybe we ought to write something out for tomorrow so we can read it to everybody," she said. Aunt Eve began to put the teacups back in the tray, and Tom stood up. He wanted to say the right thing, if only he could figure out what the right thing was. He looked at Mr. Hill. "Thank you for coming over with us," he said.

"I'm glad you asked me to," Mr. Hill said, standing up. Tom looked over at Aunt Eve. "I'm sorry," he said, though he didn't exactly know what he was sorry about.

"I'm sorry too, because I'll miss you," she said. She walked to the window and looked out at the dying day. "But you have no reason to apologize to me. It's been a fine summer, and you've made it that way. I'm sorry it's over, but it is." She turned away from the window and looked at them. "Perhaps I should apolo-

gize to you. It would make more sense. After all, I
deceived you, and kidnapped you. But I won't apologize, I've given you a hard summer, but a good one.
You're stronger and better people because of it, and
if I could live June over, I'd kidnap you again. Now,
I think you'd better go upstairs."

They left.

The statement Tom wrote for the meeting the next
morning was short, formal, and a little awkward. It
sounded like one of Mr. Eliot's editorials. It said:

> In all civilized countries it is right for guests to
> say goodbye when they leave. We are happy to
> obey that rule of civilized people. We are going
> to have to leave now. We thank you for your
> kindness and your politeness. We have been very
> happy here, and we are very glad we came, and
> we will always keep everything a secret. Thank
> you.
>
> Thomas and Sharon Inlander

After it was written, and it took Tom only a few
minutes to do it, they got ready for bed without talking. When they were in their pajamas, they went to
the top of the stairs and listened. They couldn't hear
any talk from downstairs, but they felt that Mr. Hill
was probably still there. Tom called down, "We're
all through in the bathroom, Aunt Eve."

"Thank you, Tom. I'll be up in a little while."

Tom went to his room, and Sharon followed him.
He got into bed, and she sat at the end of it. They

thought silently about what was going to happen the next morning. They heard the front door open and shut, and Aunt Eve come up the stairs. The bathroom door closed.

"They're going to be awfully surprised tomorrow when we tell them we're going. They'll probably think we're crazy," Tom said.

"They'd probably feel better if we told them we're going because we miss our parents so much," Sharon said.

"Do you?" Tom asked her.

"Do you?" she asked back.

"A little bit, once in a while," he said. "Sometimes it makes me feel bad that I don't miss them more."

"I feel the same way," Sharon said. They heard Aunt Eve come out of the bathroom, and then they heard her shut her bedroom door. Quietly, Sharon left. Tom turned out his light and tried to sleep, but he was too excited. The more he tried, the wider awake he got. Finally he got up and went barefoot downstairs and into the living room. He wanted just to sit and watch the fire die. Sharon was already there, sitting in a corner of the couch with her knees drawn up under her chin. They whispered "Hi" to each other, and Tom sat down at the other end of the couch to watch. They sat together in silence until the fire was only glowing coals. Too tired to yawn, they stood up, walked slowly out of the living room, and went upstairs. They fell asleep right away.

xx

Exile

The next morning Sharon came down for breakfast in a skirt instead of dungarees. Otherwise, everything was the same as on any other morning. Halfway through breakfast the Meeting House bell began to ring. They finished eating in a hurry, Aunt Eve and Sharon put the dishes in the sink, and they started out. On the way to the Meeting House, Tom felt in his right pants pocket to make sure the statement was still there. It was.

Mr. Simpson was standing at the Meeting House door.

"Welcome."

He made a smile and a little bow and shook Aunt Eve's hand. He started inside, stopped, turned around, and shook first Sharon's hand and then Tom's. "Welcome," he said again. "Everyone's here now."

Just before he went through the door into the Meeting House, Tom looked up. The sky was a beautiful blue, and right above his head hung a fleecy cloud, white as the whitest snow.

Aunt Eve walked down the middle aisle ahead of them, neither fast nor slow. She stopped at the second to the front pew and let Sharon slide into it ahead of her. Mr. Simpson went to the pulpit, coughed, smiled, and read "A Brief Address on the Value of Public Remarks." It went on forever.

Tom began to feel hot and a little bit sick to his stomach. A dizzy-foggy vision of Mr. Hill drifted into his mind. He saw him galloping across the island dressed like Paul Revere, shouting, "The children are going!" to old ladies in nightcaps with their heads stuck out of second-floor windows.

There was silence, and Tom realized that Mr. Simpson was through. Now he was supposed to get up and say what he had to say. His heart started gulping big swallows of blood and a chill went down his back. He got up, slid out of the pew, and walked to the pulpit. He took the statement from his pocket and smoothed it out on the lectern. While he was smoothing it, he said in a firm voice, "Thank you very much for coming here this morning." Then he read the statement. He read loudly, so that everyone would hear, and he looked up between sentences, so it wouldn't sound so short. The people were spread out in front of him like small, solitary, treeless islands in a hard brown sea. When he was through, everyone remained still. They didn't look angry, or sad, or upset, or relieved, or anything at all.

Tom began to feel a little silly just standing there. He was about to go back to his seat when Mr. Hill stood up in the back and asked if anyone had any questions he'd like to ask, or anything he'd like to say. Still there was silence. No one's face changed. Then someone spoke.

"I don't believe it."

Everyone turned that way. It was Mr. Jordan. Tom and Sharon often met him out walking in the morning, and rather liked him.

"I don't believe it. No one ever wants to leave here. It's impossible."

There was silence again.

"Does anyone have anything else to say?" Mr. Hill asked.

"It's impossible," Mr. Jordan said again, and a lone woman in the back said, "That's right, it can't be." There were sounds of agreement from various places, and then it was still again. A fly landed on the corner of Tom's paper and began to work his way toward the middle of it. Mr. Hill spoke again.

"Thank you, Tom, you may sit down until Mr. Simpson dismisses the meeting."

Tom could hardly believe that his part was over. He hesitated a moment, then left the pulpit. As he was coming around toward the middle aisle, Mr. Jordan suddenly stood up and started to slide out toward him. Tom didn't want to be grabbed, so he stopped and took a step backwards. Mr. Jordan, hurrying, got one foot caught behind him as he moved into the aisle, and fell down so hard the building shook. In the middle of the crash came the sound of a bone snapping in two.

Silence. Everyone on tiptoe.

"I've broken something."

Mr. Jordan said it as if he had just made the most important discovery he had ever made in a long and varied life.

"I've broken something." Mr. Hill was next to him now, gently feeling his left leg from the hip to the foot. He looked up at Tom. "Fetch my bag. It's next to the *Atlantic* magazines to the right of the fireplace." Tom took a quick look at Mr. Jordan, whose leg was still twisted in the pew, and then took off up the aisle. He raced out of the Meeting House, down the stairs, and along the middle of Main Street. Above him the sky was still a wonderful blue, and the sea air against his face felt clean and smelled better than anything. He went through Mr. Hill's front door without slowing down, grabbed the bag, and flew back to the Meeting House. As he ran up the stairs, he saw two men coming along the street carrying an empty stretcher between them.

Inside the building, no one seemed to have moved. It was as if they had all been waiting for a photographer to come and take their picture. Even their faces looked fixed in poses. As he went down the aisle, he saw, or perhaps he only heard or felt, a few people begin to move toward the door.

"It's impossible . . . It's impossible," Mr. Jordan was mumbling.

Tom handed Mr. Hill his bag and wished that there was something he could do to take the bewildered look off Mr. Jordan's face. Mr. Hill pushed up Mr. Jordan's left shirtsleeve and gave him a shot of something. While he was doing this, the men came puffing in with the stretcher. The Meeting House was almost empty. Two women stood near the back. Tom tried to remember their names, but couldn't. They both looked as if they wanted to help.

"It seems to be a simple fracture below the knee," Mr. Hill said to Mr. Jordan. "Nothing to be alarmed about at all. After I've set it, you can stay at my house for a few days."

"I want to go home," Mr. Jordan said. His voice was loud, but it had a dreamy quality. "Just as you say," Mr. Hill said, "but we have to go to my house anyway to set it."

Sharon was standing next to Tom now, almost touching his elbow. Mr. Hill stood up and turned toward them.

"We'll have to say goodbye here. I'll miss you."

"Maybe we'll see each other again," Sharon said. There was a lump in her throat, but she was determined not to cry. "Perhaps," he said. She wanted to put her arms around his neck, and put her head on his shoulder, hold on tight, and not open her eyes for a long restful time, but Mr. Jordan was between them. Her throat was too tight to say any more, even goodbye. She looked down at the floor. Mr. Hill put out his hand to Tom, and they shook hands firmly. "All right," he said to the men with the stretcher, and together they eased Mr. Jordan onto it, lifted it, and carried him out.

Aunt Eve stepped between Tom and Sharon and put an arm around each of them. They started out. As they passed by the two ladies in the back, she said, "You remember Mrs. Burns and Miss Dome, I'm sure. Mrs. Burns helped you with your laundry the first week you were here."

"We appreciated that very much," Tom said.

"That was very nice of you," Sharon said.

"Thank you," Tom said.

Mrs. Burns backed a step and nodded. "I only washed it, my sister ironed it."

"Yes," Miss Dome said.

"Thank you," Sharon said looking at her. "We appreciated it very much."

"We just wanted to see you close again before you go," Mrs. Burns said. "It was nice having you here."

"It was nice being here," Tom said.

"We wish you could stay. We always liked young people. I had five youngsters myself. Of course they're all gone now." Mrs. Burns smiled cheerfully. "Well, it was nice having you here."

"It was nice being here," Tom said.

Outside, the sun was bright. They squinted and started down the steps. "Too bad you aren't staying," Miss Dome said behind them. They didn't turn around. A woman began tapping on the window of a house they passed. Neither Tom nor Sharon recognized her. She stopped tapping and started waving. They waved back and smiled.

The walk to the dock passed like a dream. They waved at some more people who were waving at them, but they never stopped moving. Homer Patience met them and walked behind them down the gangplank onto the barge. The motors boomed, and with a lot of shaking and thrashing and rumbling they started moving. Tom and Sharon stood at the back and watched the island go away. It got smaller fast.

After a while Aunt Eve came with a small black box camera in her hand and gave it to Tom. "Mr. Rice asked me to give this to you and tell you he was sorry you didn't have time to come and see his other cameras and his darkroom."

"Thank you."

Tom took the camera in his hands and looked at it. It was old, but very well kept, and he was glad to have it.

"Would you tell him thank you for me, and tell him I'm sorry I didn't get to see his other cameras?"

Tom bit his lip and turned. Holding the camera tight, he watched the island and began to think of all the things he'd planned to do but hadn't done. He'd planned to hunt wild cranberries, he'd planned to make a really good shell collection with all the shells labeled, he'd planned to build a beach house out of driftwood, and mark some trails through the woods, and dry some birchbark to make scrolls for writing on, and make a bow and flinthead arrows, and make the roof on their fort waterproof. And he hadn't done any of these things. He felt like a man going into exile.

"Exile," Sharon thought to herself, watching the island get smaller. "It's just like going into exile." She thought of Mr. Hill, who had been as kind to her as her father, had understood her without making her afraid, and had told her the truth, clearly and gently. Tears came to her eyes and blurred what she could still see of the island.

"I'll never see it again," she said quietly to herself. "I'll never see it again."

After a while they ate some sandwiches, and then pretty soon the barge bumped tight against the end of a long wooden dock. Near the dock was a big shed. A blacktop road ran from the dock past the shed and curved inland between green fenced fields before it disappeared into the woods. The pastures to the left and right of the road came almost down to the sea. They were back where they had been that gusty night when Aunt Eve had awakened them in the car, given them raincoats, and taken them across the water.

They wanted desperately to go back to the island for just a day or two longer.

Manhattan

It was early afternoon when Aunt Eve drove them away from the dock and along the curving road which led through the woods to the main highway. At sunset they stopped at a Howard Johnson's for dinner. Aunt Eve in a dark green silk suit, Sharon in a white skirt and red blouse, and Tom in a sweat shirt and dungarees, sat together at a window and looked at the mountains and talked quietly. They didn't mention the island.

When they got back into the car again, it was dark.

"I think you two should get married," Sharon said after they had been driving for a while. She had been holding that sentence back since the middle of July, and it was a relief to get it out.

"I think so too," Aunt Eve said right away. "It's foolish for us to be living separately."

"Then why don't you?"

"There aren't any good reasons, Sharon . . . Do you think I should propose to him when I get back?"

"Yes. You're both stuck on the island anyway, so you might just as well live together and try to enjoy it more. You love each other."

"That's right, we do," Aunt Eve said. "And we are both stuck, as you say." She smiled. "You're a direct young woman, aren't you? Where'd you learn that?"

Sharon didn't answer. She just smiled.

Tom leaned forward—he was sitting next to the door—and looked at Aunt Eve. "Do you believe in God?"

She glanced over to him. "Is that an important question to you?"

"Yes, I think so."

"I've always believed that there was something holy in the world."

"Why?"

"Because of people like you and Sharon, who love life in the world more than they fear death."

They were silent, and in a while Sharon fell asleep. Soon Tom did too. He woke up once in the middle of the night when they stopped for gas, and then later they both woke up and watched the dawn. They stopped for breakfast at another Howard Johnson's, and by half past ten they were in New York.

The city looked the same, but they felt strange in it. The people moving along the streets had the same blank faces they remembered from the Meeting House.

Aunt Eve parked in front of their apartment building, and pulled on the hand brake. They began to be afraid that someone would recognize them and call the police and catch her, but Aunt Eve seemed to be enjoying the risk.

"Will you still write to us?" Sharon asked.

"After a while," Aunt Eve said.

"It's not that we want any money from you or anything," Tom said. "It's just . . ." He didn't quite know how to say it. There were tears in his eyes, and they made everything look foggy.

"I know you don't want anything from me."

"We love you," Sharon said, looking at the floor of the car.

"And I love you," Aunt Eve said. "And since that's the highest thing anybody can say to anybody, let's not say anything else . . . It's enough. Go home."

She reached over in front of Sharon to open the door, and as she did, Sharon brushed her cheek with a kiss. Then the door was open, and Tom and Sharon were on the sidewalk, and the car was driving away.

And then it was gone.

Another Letter

"We had a very good summer with friends."

That was all Tom and Sharon would say about where they had been and what had happened to them. They were questioned by policemen and psychologists and teachers and classmates and newspaper reporters and relatives and their mother and father, and all they would say was, "We had a very good summer with friends."

Then one Sunday morning at breakfast their father

looked up from his toast and said to their mother, "Well, they came back stronger people than they were when they left, so I guess we'd better let them keep their secret. Pass the strawberry jam, please."

And as far as their parents were concerned, that was that. Neither their mother nor their father ever asked them another question about their summer disappearance. That made it easier for them to keep their secret from everyone else, including an all-too-real aunt who had a thousand crazy ideas about what had happened to them, and couldn't stop trying to get them to tell her.

A year later their mother had a baby girl. They insisted that she be named Eve, and their parents gave in. The day Eve and her mother came home from the hospital, a brief letter arrived, addressed to Tom and Sharon.

Dear Tom and Sharon,

I'm delighted about your new sister. I dropped into the hospital the other day disguised as a grandmother and saw her. Thank you for naming her Eve—I've always liked the name. Perhaps some day you'll let me steal her, for a piece of time.

Love from,
Aunt Eve

Tom and Sharon thought that was a fine idea.